Holistic
Healing

Published by Winco Books India
(An Imprint of Winco Publishing)
Kottayam 686575, Kerala, India
wincobooks@gmail.com
wincoindia.com

First Winco Edition 2019

HOLISTIC HEALING
The Karmu System of Holistic Health and Wellness

ISBN 978-81-933571-3-2

Cover Design by Baiju Gopal, Civet
Design and typesetting by Winco Publishing Services

Holistic Healing

THE KARMU SYSTEM
OF HOLISTIC HEALTH AND WELLNESS

ᘓ ❦ ᘔ

Dr. RICARDO FRAZER

WINCO
BOOKS

Dedication

This book is dedicated to **Edgar H. Warner (Swami Muktananda Karmu)** as a tribute to the work he completed and the greatness he achieved. Karmu created a Foundation designed to provide funds and other things proper and necessary in furtherance of the creation of a universal spiritual community. The purpose was to promote universal peace and the study, practice and observance of spirit. A major goal was to provide care, sustenance, shelter and clothing to those in need. Karmu's plan for a Foundation was formulated and formative steps were taken; however, full operation was never achieved. It lives on in the hearts and minds of those of us who believe in him and his divine mission.

CB CB CB

Acknowledgements

Very special thanks to **Dr. Curtis Todd** who made major and significant contributions. This book would not exist without his generosity. I am grateful to the students of Karmu for their contributions (Guru's are known by the works of their students). I am also grateful to the students I have had over the years who contributed to this writing in a variety of ways.

THUS SPOKE KARMU

"I am my brother's keeper; if he's cold, I shall warm him; if he's hungry, I shall feed him. If he's unloved, I shall love him, and I shall hold him in my breast and make him me. Therefore we are both two-in-one, one-in-two. A part of God! That is the philosophy of life. If you follow this philosophy, the world is yours. Your whole body will sing – I rest my case!"

ɑ ɑ ɑ

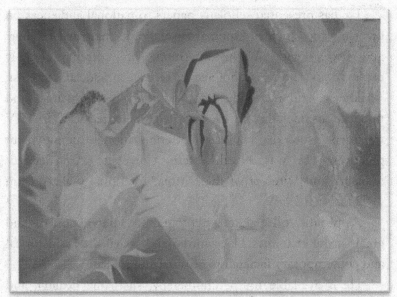

"Karmu Healer" oil painting on canvas by Dr. Ricardo Frazer

Dr. Ricardo Frazer

Dr. RICARDO FRAZER is a Professor of Psychology in the Division of Social Sciences at Atlanta Metropolitan State College. He holds degrees from Bowling Green State University (Ph.D., M.A., Industrial/Organizational Psychology), Harvard University (Ed.M., Counseling and Consulting Psychology), and the  University of Connecticut (B.A., Psychology, B.S., Environmental Horticulture). He is a Licensed Board Certified Psychology Diplomate and was elected a Fellow of the Linnean Society of London in 2003.

He has presented scholarly papers to national audiences on diverse topics such as Optimal Psychology, Shamanic Healing, and Psychological Wellness. Among his current scholarly explorations are psychological resiliency, social interest, worldview, and racial identity. Additional research areas and publications include the use of silver nano particles in HIV treatment protocols, and racial discrimination in employment practices. He was Northwestern University Art Services Manager and Director of the Dittmar Memorial Gallery from 1992 through 1999.

A prolific oil painter, photographer, percussionist, and guitarist, he examines black music and visual art as historical and contemporary facilitators of ritual and trance.

He is available for psychotherapy, shamanic healing, and consultation at *rfrazer007@gmail.com*

ભ ભ ભ

CONTENTS

FOREWORD

DR. JOHN THEKKEDAM
(SWAMI SNEHANANDA JYOTI)

AS BACKGROUND to this Foreword, I want to describe two scenarios. One about Sigmund Freud and the other about Brian Weiss.

1. I want to highlight a startling fact about Sigmund Freud, the father of modern psychology and the founder of Psychoanalysis, and Brian L. Weiss, M.D., who graduated from Columbia University, and was Chairman of the Department of Psychiatry at the Mount Sinai Medical Center in Miami, Florida, USA, when he began to delve into unorthodox parapsychology and, published his book, *Many Lives, Many Masters*, in 1988. Freud psychoanalyzed himself. Making significant contributions to psychology, he gave psychology respectability and credibility in the field of social sciences.

From the writings of Ernest Jones (*The Life and Work of Sigmund Freud*, in three volumes: a definitive and authoritative classic), a close friend, associate, and faithful disciple of Freud in his last fifteen years, and Eric Fromm (*Sigmund Freud's Mission – An Analysis of His Personality and Influence*), a great psychologist who was analyzed by Freud's own daughter, Anna Freud, one can glean data to arrive at the conclusion that Freud was a narcissistic personality in that he used his friends and followers to advance his own goals; his friendship mostly ended when he had no use for his friends. Freud could have used a good dose of psychoanalysis himself. The creator of psychoanalysis did not use it wisely himself.

2. After getting no success after 18 months of conventional psychotherapy, Weiss through hypnotic regression and analysis got into the past lives of his patient, and removed the causative factors or symptoms that terribly disturbed the patient. He had no scientific explanation for the recovery his patient experienced. I have brought in Freud and Weiss just to make the point that even though we have made great strides and inroads into psychology, we still do not have explanations for certain curative factors or lack thereof. It is in this context we need to look at Karmu's healing system of psychological and physical healing.

I have been exploring the mysteries of the human mind and the soul through spirituality, literature, philosophy, theology, comparative religion, history, and psychology for over 60 adult years in India and the USA. Of over 45 years in psychotherapy and psychological evaluation, I spent 30 years in the USA after receiving PhD in Clinical Psychology from Saint Louis University, Saint Louis, USA. After long years of practicing psychotherapy and teaching psychology, I came to the conclusion that human mind is a vast and mysterious unconscious, as vast as the cosmos, into which we have only a very small glimpse. The human mind is still a very big enigma.

Weiss stated that "there is far too much about the human mind that is far beyond our comprehension." Weiss stated that in his patient's regression, she served as a "conduit for information from highly evolved 'spirit entities', and through them she revealed many of the secrets of life and death" that led to her healing. He speculated that "Perhaps under hypnosis, Catherine (his patient) was able to focus on the part of her subconscious mind that stored actual life memories, or she tapped into what the psychoanalyst Carl Jung termed the collective unconscious, the energy source that surrounds us and contains the memories of the entire human race."

Holistic Healing: The Karmu System of Holistic Health and Wellness by Ricardo Frazer, PhD, integrates the healing of the body, mind, and the spirit. The Karmu system of healing is more akin to that of shamanism. Karmu had an extraordinary empathetic ability to get into the minds and hearts of the persons who went to him for help and healing. His approach is idiographic; his case histories may not be replicated, and may not lend to statistical analysis and conclusions. He used his own unique charism to make people at ease. Not having any formal training in psychology, he won their hearts over, and developed healing (therapeutic) alliance to effect the healing. Unlike traditional psychotherapists who have a fixed fee for their services and hence bound by certain standards of their professional certification and license, he worked out of his innate wisdom that came spontaneously from his gut level. Solicitude and concern for the well-being of his clients overruled other considerations.

Karmu believed his own body, for instance, could transmit healing power to others. He employed with ease aspects of parapsychology such as clairvoyance, telepathy, and entering the sub-conscious mind. He would enter one's sub-conscious mind, for instance, to boost one's self-esteem. He would use acupressure to activate pressure points to alleviate symptoms. He would employ massage to clear knots and blocks in the body. He would suggest herbs and herbal medicines for refreshing oneself. In all this, his aim was to restore the body, mind, and spirit of every client to a tension-free, relaxed, and fully-functioning state as testified by many persons, including Dr. Frazer, who benefited from his healing system. Dr. Frazer did an excellent job in presenting "The Karmu System of Healing" to the world.

ೞ ೞ ೞ

01

INTRODUCTION
TO KARMU

I WAS a master's degree student studying Counseling and Consulting Psychology at Harvard University when I met Karmu. I was embedded in the world of standard American medicine and scientific approaches to knowledge. I had received an introduction to alternative medicine because I once visited a homeopathic practitioner who suggested that I adopt a diet that he considered to be healthier than the one I was on at that time.

So I knew that there were alternatives to the standard medicine I had grown up with, but a couple of visits to a homeopath were the extent of my knowledge in this area. I knew nothing about the approach to healing that Karmu was practicing and I had never heard of or met a faith healer. My first meeting with him was a major eye opener. I did not know that men like Karmu existed. He was completely outside the realm of my experience and imagination.

I visited him as a last resort because I was having a health crisis and was desperate for help. At that point I was willing to try almost anything to get better so that I could get on with my master's degree studies. The day I visited him, I was in physical pain, in a stupor, lethargic, and experiencing pervasive brain fog. The day after I visited him, I was energetic, clear headed, enthusiastic, and eager to get back to work. A transformation of my health happened in less than 24 hours.

This experience convinced me that I needed to find out how Karmu "healed" me (after I had spent four days in a hospital). Over the course of the next four years, I spent a great deal of time "at the feet of the guru." I loved it! So much so, that I stopped thinking about my original plan to pursue doctoral studies and instead just lived in the moment, happy to be around Karmu.

During the time spent with him I learned that after a career as an automobile mechanic, he became a healer who utilized a broad spectrum of natural techniques, including simple medicines, diet, fasting, massage, personal counseling, herbal, mineral, and externally-applied compounds to cure ailments.

Numerous anecdotes, some garnered from Karmu himself, suggested that not only was he a healer, but also a priest, psychological counselor, political activist, mystic, and sage. Like the indigenous shaman, he mediated life and death through his ability to enter trance-like states. One of his gifts was the ability to alter the energy state of another person. He achieved this by his touch, by his presence, or through objects energized with his energy. He stated that his practice was a combination of African and Asian healing techniques that he learned from his West Indian mother, his "Ethiopian Jewish" father (the Rabbi Shabu) and from other healers including Dr. Buzzard healers and Sufi masters like Murshid Sam Lewis.

As a Harvard University student studying counseling, I was fascinated with this opportunity to gain further insight into the healing process and the process of change. The years that I spent "at the feet" of Karmu left me inspired by his wisdom, knowledge, compassion, and courage. He said he healed others by getting in tune with them, penetrating their subconscious mind, taking their pain into his body, and dispersing the pain into the cosmic arena. "Show them that they're loved unconditionally and make them laugh," were some of the words he used. Every visit with him was a lesson in health, politics, and mystical reality. I eventually completed the Karmu Foundation certification course in "Psychic, Herbal, and Alternative Healing" on July 19, 1981.

I completed this course by visiting him a couple days a week, starting in the fall of 1979. Those seeking his services during my time there included psychiatrists, nurses, ministers, drug addicts, alcoholics, lawyers, cab drivers, veterans of foreign wars, college students, and so on. In Karmu's words, "there is never a dull moment here." Some of the more well known visitors were people like R.D. Laing, Andrew Weil, Ram Dass, Malcolm X, Elijah Mohammed, Sufi Sam, David McClelland, and Alan Ginsberg, to name a few.

On many occasions, Karmu could be seen bringing himself and others to states of ecstasy using his highly developed charisma, his "gift of gab" and his ability to provoke laughter and merriment. Frequently, he would appear to drop off into deep sleep, returning fresh with energy for another ritualistic episode, and awaken talking of "having left his body."

The current writing was encouraged and endorsed by Karmu and written in hopes of capturing some of the charisma, generosity, compassion and wisdom that he shared. I believe that in the next twenty years we will see a transition in American healthcare whereby there will be more healthcare providers like Karmu extending the work of standard medical doctors. There will be more natural and non-physician healthcare extenders providing healthcare and operating outside of mainstream medicine.

One factor leading to this change is the need to reduce the financial burden of health care. This transition has been in motion for a long time. Karmu and others like him are trendsetters for this health care revolution. In time, the uneasy coexistence between traditional health care providers and the alternative practitioners that complement the traditional mainstream system, will transform into greater compatibility.

I challenge and encourage the reader to remain open – suspend, if not abandon preconceived or prejudicial anticipations. May his life's work continue to guide those in need. The assembling of the fifteen chapters are deliberate. They have been carefully considered and constructed in content and form. Just as holistic health and wellness is a journey, this introduction to Karmu is a journey as well.

From the initial introduction to his world, to the final reflections about his life, an intentional exploration is systematically mapped that hopefully insures that the novice learner seeking a path, to the scholarly academician, and the skilled practitioner expanding a rich knowledge base, will receive valuable insights.

As you embrace this book, there must be a suspension or a shedding of old skin or garments, if not a partial abandonment of notions around what is disease, wellness, and how we are healed. Within the healing profession, as well as in the lay communities of practitioners, varied frameworks and strategies offer different pathways to wellness. Indigenous methods of achieving physical, psychological and spiritual well-being have been documented, and passed forward through oral traditions. The well coined adage that "wellness is more than the absence of disease" has been a tipping point in our efforts. We continue to ponder the definitions and understanding of wellness, disease and healing. This questioning must never lose its voice!

What does it truly mean to experience wellness? Our perspectives must continue to grow, evolve and untold ones must be brought to light. Shamanic healing shines brightly. We must rid ourselves of constructs that have not served us well and those that only mask underlining disease and unhealthy patterns. We must journey to the core and not become fixated on treating only the symptoms of discomfort. There are numerous conduits to healing and sustained wellness. This book is yet another perspective. We challenge you. Disrobe. Come and discover Karmu!

ෟ ෟ ෟ

02

DISCOVERING
THE HEALER AND GURU

MY FIRST meeting with Karmu was in the fall of 1979. I now suspect that my meeting with him was connected to a deep-seated need within me for spiritual growth and development. A need I did not recognize at that time. He and I lived about five city blocks apart from each other in Cambridge, Massachusetts, but I didn't know him. I was having severe muscle spasms in my lower back at the time and was deciding what to do about it.

One day while walking down Massachusetts Avenue on my way to the Harvard University Hospital, I saw a guy that I had met years before when we were undergraduates at the University of Connecticut. I told him about my back pain and he suggested that I see a local healer named Karmu. The guy was Latino and visiting a healer was a very natural thing for him. I didn't have that mindset. In my mind I was having a serious problem and needed some urgent medical attention, not a faith healer. So when he gave me Karmu's phone number and told me Karmu was a Curandero, I put the number in my pocket with no plan to use it.

That day I made my way to the Harvard Medical Clinic and was told by a medical doctor to simply sleep on a firm surface. The doctor made no other recommendations. That night I found myself in excruciating pain and in a severe pain crisis. At about 3:00 am in the morning I got out of bed, fell to the floor, and could not get up. I laid there on my bedroom floor, in pain, unable to move, until my housemate woke up, about four hours later, and heard me calling out in distress.

I was taken in a police car to the same Harvard Hospital I had visited earlier. I spent the next four days in a hospital bed taking various medications to control pain and relax muscles. When I was released from the hospital I was out of my pain crisis and I walked home in a drug stupor. Instead of excruciating pain, I was experiencing dull aching pain, along with brain fog. When I arrived home I located the phone number I had been given earlier by my former classmate and gave Karmu a phone call.

THE PHONE CALL

Ricardo: Hello, may I speak to Karmu?

Karmu: I'm Karmu, who's speaking?

Ricardo: My name is Ricardo, a friend of mine told me that you're a healer.

Karmu: How old are you, 28?

Ricardo: No, I'm 29.

Karmu: So I lie a little. I've been known to heal all diseases known to man, what can I do for you?

Ricardo: I've been having really bad pain in my lower back, is that something that you deal with?

Karmu: We'll have you pain free overnight.

Ricardo: That would really impress me.

Karmu: Why do you speak the Queen's English so well?

Ricardo: I'm a college student.

Karmu: Come on over, we'll have you running and jumping before you know it. You'll have zuk and wok, glide in your stride, and soon you'll be doing Kung Fu like Fu Man Chu.

Ricardo: Do you mean come over right now? How did you know my age?

Karmu: I know things. Yeah, right now unless you're gonna be busy running track.

Ricardo: No, I'm not going to be running any time soon.

Karmu spoke fast and I was having trouble keeping up, but the warmth in his voice was palpable and welcoming. When he gave me his address I quickly realized I could be there in a matter of minutes. My brain was still very foggy, but I had no problem locating his house. The pain in my back was really saying something, "You're gonna be lying around the apartment for a while, so don't make any plans. Reading and writing, no, none of that either, I've got other plans for you. We're gonna sit and watch television. School work – forget about it. We're putting college on hold."

He lived in a working class neighborhood, in a green house that he owned. The street he lived on ran parallel to Massachusetts Avenue (one street over). The connecting street was Hancock Street. The embedded dirt and thick grime on the pavement made it apparent that Hancock Street was a high traffic area. It was daytime, but the Plough & Shield bar on the corner of Mass Ave and Hancock was in full swing. The door was open, I could see people inside. They were talking loud enough for me to make out conversations. Blues music was being playing on a jukebox. It seemed rowdy in there and the energy felt angry and unfriendly towards "outsiders".

Karmu lived on the second floor of a two-level house right on the corner of Putnam Street and Green Street. The highly worn stairs up to the second floor creaked with anticipation as I walked up. If those stairs could talk, I'd hear all about an army of people who had beat them down. I was surprised to find that the door at the top of the stairs was unlocked, so I just walked in.

"Come on back here," A loud voice boomed out. "What took you so long?"

I was surprised to see a black man sitting on his bed as I walked into a small bedroom. I had not expected a member of my own race. His voice had not given away his racial identity. A massive, shirt-less, Buddha-like figure was sitting on the edge of his bed with his feet on the floor watching television. He had big arms, powerful shoulders, large muscles, and a large belly. His hair was closely cut and a little bit of gray was cropping out on the sides.

He talked with his hands and smiled a lot. "You look like a movie star," he said. "No, you look like nine movie stars. Soon, we'll have you glowing in the dark just like me. Here, take this bottle of blue medicine and go to take a bath. When the bathwater gets cool, heat it up again. Soak for about an hour. There are paper towels in there you can use to dry off."

"He acts like he knows me," were my immediate thoughts.

The bedroom was small and there was a bench across from Karmu's double bed. Over the head of the bed were a couple shelves. On one self was a turntable that wasn't hooked up to any stereo, on the other was a row of books. I could make out one of the book titles since I recognized it – *Memories, Dreams and Reflections* by Carl Jung. The room was fairly sparse – a bed, a dresser, a small refrigerator. A donation box shaped like a pyramid hung on the wall behind the bench. A few children's toys were on the floor in the corner.

Karmu handed me a wine bottle with purple liquid inside. He spoke quickly, and some of the words got by me, but I got the gist of his instructions and followed them. I thought to myself, "I don't even know him and he's letting me use his bathtub. Okay, why not, we'll give this a shot. He seems like a nice guy."

The bathroom was small and I was immediately struck by a large mural on the wall the tub was up against. It was a painting of a tree with lots of people coming out of it as if they were growing out of the tree. The mural was composed of very bright colors. There was something organic about the image – a picture I would characterize as "new age". It was an amazing image that I had not seen before. The artwork was striking and extremely well done. I felt that someone had put lots of time and care into rendering it.

After an hour or so of soaking in the bathtub, I returned to the bedroom to find that a guy and a girl had arrived, and they were sitting and talking. When I walked into the room Karmu instructed me to remove my shirt and sit on his bed. He rubbed some liquid ointment in his hands and began to massage my neck and back while talking about the benefits of blue and white medicine. Blue medicine was a solution of potassium permanganate that I had soaked in; he said it would draw toxins out of my body.

White medicine was a mixture of olive oil, peppermint, camphor, wintergreen, and other fragrant oils. Karmu talked as he skillfully massaged my head, neck, and back. While he massaged he described what he was doing. He talked about manipulating trigger points, stimulating my meridian system, energizing my chakras, and removing blockage in major energy centers, especially my neck. He tapped on some points and rubbed others, and inquired about the amount of pressure I was experiencing. While he massaged he explained that he was using personally designed techniques to free up my blocked energy, move the life-force around and activate more energy flow in my body.

Karmu: You're a bright guy, a golden child. I think I'll make you an SS, a special student. I hope you're taking notes because we have a lot of ground to cover in a short amount of time. Right now I'm penetrating your subconscious with a DPE, a definite plus element, elevating your consciousness, and taking away your pain. I take your pain into my body and disperse it out into the cosmic arena. It really hurts.

Ricardo: I don't think you want my pain.

Karmu: I can handle it, handle it all. One week ago a woman arrived here all the way from Puerto Rico. She had a rare disease that no one could heal. She heard about me from healers on the island. They sent her to me. Her hands were cramped up for years. She was practically an invalid. I healed her in a week. It hurt me real bad. But I'm a bad dude, a dangerous cat. No pain can phase me. I'm up to the task. I rest my case.

I didn't know what to believe. Taking my pain into his body… penetrating my subconscious… dispersing pain into the cosmic arena. It all seemed pretty unbelievable to me.

Ricardo: How do you penetrate the subconscious mind?

Karmu: I get to know you. Who you are and how you think. I do it fast, real fast; you won't even know that it's happening. It's called hypnosis.

Ricardo: Well, I'd like to learn more about that. I'm studying psychology. Hypnosis is right up my alley.

Karmu: I knew we had a thinker here, come by often, as often as you like. I'll turn you into a TFC – top flight cat. You've got potential, but you're stiff, like a newly pressed shirt, we need to loosen you up.

I didn't quite care for the reference to me as a stiff shirt. I was skeptical about Karmu and his brand of healing, but I was eager to learn anything I could. The vibe coming from him felt genuine and caring. But a black healer – that was a first for me. Never mind a fast-talking black guy that wasn't making the kind of rational sense my college-trained mind was accustomed to hearing. The two other people in the room were paying attention to Karmu from time to time and at other times talking freely as if they were at home in their living room.

Karmu continued to massage me and provide explanations of what he was doing. At times he would explain something to the people in the room or instruct them to eat some soup or drink some red medicine. Karmu was continually orchestrating the activity of everyone around him.

After the massage I was instructed to soak my feet in a solution of hot water and blue medicine. I was told that this was another detoxification. Then I drank a solution of black medicine from a small paper cup. Karmu told me it was his special blend of herbs. Then I was given a bowl of hot vegetable soup that Karmu said a chicken had been "dragged through" – there was a lot of onions and garlic in it. After eating I hung out for a couple hours or so. Karmu drank red medicine – his blend of wine, fruit juices and herbs, and offered it to other people who arrived. It didn't take long before many people had arrived and there was a party atmosphere in the bedroom.

The energy in the room kept getting higher and higher. He laughed, joked, watched television, answered the phone, it was just crazy. I was mesmerized by all of what was going on and having fun at the same time. When I was ready to leave Karmu gave me a large brown bag filled with bottles of blue and black medicine and instructed me to bathe regularly in the blue solution and to continue soaking my feet and drinking black medicine. We talked about the kind of foods I eat and he made recommendations.

Then he told me what he usually charged for his services, but commented that he knew I didn't have much money and that I could make whatever donation I felt I could handle. I found him to be gracious and extremely generous. I wasn't the kind of person who warmed up to people very quickly. I had just met Karmu, but already I felt like a member of his family.

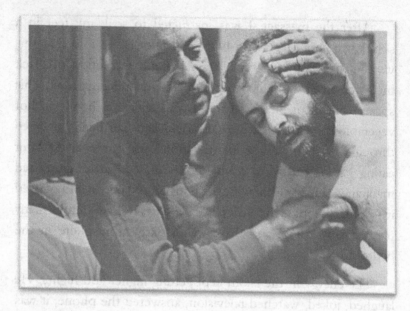

Karmu healing a client…

ɔ ɔ ɔ

03

WALKING ON WATER AND THROUGH WALLS

WE ARE moving even closer to the Karmu experience. It is presented in question and answer format in an effort to provide a more intimate view of Karmu through his own words.

The day after my first visit with Karmu, I woke up feeling like a million dollar man – I was pain free. I could hardly believe it. There was no fog in my brain and I felt like a new man. How did that happen? What did Karmu do to affect this change?

I had been in excruciating pain followed by extreme discomfort and a drug stupor. I expected to be miserable for a long time to come and had been advised by my medical doctor to continue taking my pain and muscle relaxing medication for at least another month. The fog in my brain alone was depressing. Here I was, a high-need-achiever in the middle of an academic semester and eager to get back to work, to compete, and succeed. I definitely did not want to sit around taking prescription drugs. It was my first semester in college and my anxiety level was high. The anxiety alone may have helped trigger the muscle spasms in my lower back – I don't know. What I didn't expect was to be clear-headed and pain-free a day after visiting Karmu and be ready to get back to work.

I went back to school that day. Some of my classmates had missed me and couldn't believe I had just spent four days in a hospital bed. So I offered to sell them my pain and muscle relaxing drugs, jokingly. They responded by harassing me about trying to push drugs on campus. I was so amazed by how good I felt that I decided to get back to Karmu's house as soon as possible so I could begin to make sense of my healing. Finding out how he healed people seemed just as important to me as master's degree study at Harvard University.

When I arrived back at his house a few days later, I met his live-in assistant in the kitchen. I asked her if Karmu was in and she sent me to his room. She had been out of town, visiting her family during my first visit. She was blond, with blue eyes – she was attractive and seemed socially withdrawn. She seemed friendly, but highly suspicious. I learned later from Karmu that she had become deeply troubled by bad experiences she had while serving in the military. He did not say what she had experienced and it was easy to see that she took B.S. from nobody. She seemed very intense so I didn't say much to her and walked down the hallway to Karmu's bedroom.

"Look at you, walking straight and tall," said Karmu as I walked in the room. "You came in here looking like a wounded puppy, now you look like a dozen movie stars. How can we lose with the system we use? I knew you were coming by today. Take that bottle of medicine and take another blue medicine bath."

Ricardo: I'm not sure I need it Karmu, I said, I'm feeling great.

Karmu: Well, take one anyway, he said, I want you to fly high. You're a VDC, a very decent cat.

Ricardo: How did you know I was coming by, Karmu?

I decided to follow up on his comment.

Karmu: Oh, we know things around here, was his only reply. Take a good hot bath, but don't fill the tub too high. When you get straight 'A's at Harvard, you'll mention my name.

Ricardo: Don't worry Karmu, I said, I've got your back. How did you know I went to Harvard?

Karmu: Oh, you've got question, that's just what we like around here, but don't fret it lad, we do our homework around here too, he proclaimed. When you finish your bath I've got something for you to read. I want you to tell me what you think.

After returning from my bath I received another back massage and drank some black medicine followed up with some red medicine. Then he gave me a newspaper article to read. I was expecting to read something about psychology or health, instead the article was about Israel bombing a Palestinian settlement. When I finished reading I said it was a sibling rivalry between brothers that now hate each other. I told him that I didn't really understand the very complex politics, but I thought the conflict had ancient roots.

Karmu: Oh, it's much more than that, he said.

What followed was a long rant about the United States and the British creating a Jewish state, ousting Palestinian people and maintaining a military outpost in the Middle East.

Karmu: How much do you know about these things, he asked.

Ricardo: Not much, I said, I'm pretty naive about these issues.

Karmu: Well, I'll fill you in, he said. You need to know these things. Forewarned is forearmed.

Ricardo: Well, fill me in, I said, I'm eager to learn as much as I can.

Karmu: Have you read Howard Zinn? He has been here. He wrote a great history book. How about Noam Chomsky?

Ricardo: I know of them, but I have not read their work.

Karmu: Well, keep coming around, there's a lot you need to know. By the way, you should take my class it's called psychic, herbal and alternative healing. The cost is 250 dollars. You can pay in installments. Let me know when you're ready to start.

Ricardo: Sounds good to me, Karmu, I'll let you know when I'm ready. Then we both laughed.

Karmu: You'll be a bad dude when you leave here, just like me . . . you'll be dangerous, he said.

Ricardo: I can go for dangerous, but we're not going to blow anything up, are we? I replied.

Karmu: Oh, you've got jokes too, I like that. We're just trying to make people more aware of what's going on so things might get a little bit better in this country, especially for the black man. It sure is rough out here for a black person.

Ricardo: You telling me!

Karmu: Just last week, one of my black patients lost his job because he married a white woman.

Ricardo: How do you know that was the reason, there are lots of reasons for getting fired.

Karmu: Oh, his boss warned him not to do it. She was a pretty lass too, beautiful, tall, great legs. They came by here and we talked about it. I warned them myself. White men don't want to see that. They get real jealous. In this country a black man is not supposed to be with a white woman. You can still get killed for that. But they were in love. I could see the trouble brewing. Now he's out of a job.

Ricardo: It's 1979 and that's still going on.

Karmu: Everywhere! North and South, East and West! Unless a black man wants to hold is head down, lay low and hide out, he better not get with a white woman.

Ricardo: How long has your lady friend been around, Karmu?

Karmu: Oh, she's been here a couple years. I helped her get back on her feet after the military abused her, and then she started helping out around here. She remodeled this whole apartment, built the back room and repaired the back stairs. She's got excellent skills. I taught her how to get along with people. You should have seen her when she first came. She thought the FBI was trying to kill her. Now she's doing great and I can't get her to leave. I've told her she needs to move on so I think she's making plans. She's been mending things with her family lately.

Karmu: Have you seen your grandmother lately?

Ricardo: No, I haven't seen her in years. She's an energetic ambitious woman, but I don't think she's been doing too well lately. Why did you bring up my grandmother?

Karmu: I've been picking up on her. How's her health been lately?

Ricardo: It hasn't been too good for years. She been dealing with diabetes most of her life. I don't really know how she's doing; it's a long time since I last saw her.

Karmu: Now may be the time. I've got a special clay-based poultice here. Have her use it on her feet. It was designed for horses, but it works well on people. Look under my bed, there's a box of coins. Take one and keep it on you. If you don't find a coin take a safety pin. It doesn't matter, as long as it's metal. These metal pieces are collecting my vibration.

Ricardo: How will that help me, Karmu?

Karmu: What matters is that it works. You want to keep my energy with you wherever you go. It will keep you safe and protect you. I'll give you some of my hair later. That works too. It's all about energy, mine is higher. When I was a baby my parents would use me to heal people. If someone was sick they would get to hold me for a while. Their sickness would go away. I've known I had this ability all my life. When I was a young man I walked on water without falling in, it was a pond, and I walked across it.

Ricardo: You walked on water? That violates the laws of physics. What did you have on your feet, jets?

Karmu: "No rubber boots. It was raining so I had my boots on. Many people saw it. I wasn't alone at the time.

Ricardo: I don't know anyone that can walk on water Karmu but I have heard that Jesus Christ did it.

Karmu: Well it was Christ-like. It's a gift. Did you eat yet? How about some soup, it's good, real good. Onions, garlic, ginger, yams, and a chicken was dragged through it. It was made yesterday so it had time to gel. Soup needs time to come together. It's like medicine when you make it right, but it has to sit for a while to come together. I make really good soup, well my people make it now. Now and then I have to re-train them. You hungry?

I didn't know what to make of what Karmu had said about walking on water. It was stunning to hear such things and I didn't know what more to say about it, even though it stayed on my mind. I probably dropped into a stupor. I suspect he sense my trance-like state and continued with that mode of talk.

Karmu: Did you know I visit people in their dreams? I had a patient who was dealing with epilepsy. He was taking a whole shelf of medications. I changed his diet, put him on the proper foods, and took him off all his medication. I got him doing my exercises, and put him through my whole regime. One night in his sleep he dreamed he was falling off a mountain. I came to him in his dream and caught him before he hit the ground. The next day he came to see me and told me about the dream. I told him I already knew about it. He never had another seizure.

I just sat there in his presence not knowing what to say. My eyes were probably pretty wide with a puzzled look on my face. I was trying to make some sense of it, but couldn't get my head around his statements.

Karmu: Did I tell you I walk through walls?

Ricardo: How do you walk through walls, Karmu?

At that moment a beautiful woman walked in the bedroom. She looked very unique and had a serene peaceful aura about her. I thought to myself "there is something special and unusual about her." She had soft straight hair that was parted in the middle and tied back in a bun. Were I to guess I would say she was Black, White, and Native American. She was a Cherokee

Catawba teacher and healer named Dhyani Fisher Ywahoo.

I was already in somewhat of a daze and in a moments time two highly spiritual people were laughing and having an unusual conversation that I could barely comprehend. So I just sat there feeling the vibe. I couldn't grasp the content. It was like being transported to another time and place. They talked about animals turning into people, and people turning into animals, people flying through the air like birds. I sat and listened for a while. Then I got the feeling that this was a personal conversation and that they needed space. These thoughts entered my mind in such a vivid way that I knew it was time to leave. So I politely mentioned that I had work to do and move on.

Karmu feeding a dog

ভ ভ ভ

04

DREAMS, THOUGHTS AND BELIEFS

WE TRAVELED the world, far and near in our conversations and thoughts. The course of enlightenment had no beginning or ending, no top, nor bottom.

Ricardo: Karmu, tell us about dreams. There seems to be a lot of mystery surrounding the topic of dreams. What is your understanding of dreams?

Karmu: When the conscious mind is at rest the subconscious mind brings up things that you would like to have happen or things you've seen in the past, or something you're going to see in the future. There are people who can look into themselves and interpret the dreams.

Ricardo: Identify the meaning?

Karmu: Right, I had a dream of meeting a person in a certain act at a certain time, three years ago. It actually happened. A woman passed me some pills from behind a bar. When it happened I told her about the dream.

Ricardo: So there's a certain predictive quality about certain dreams. One might be able to see into future occurrences.

Karmu: Positively.

Ricardo: What is man's purpose on Earth?

Karmu: To live in harmony with the Earth like the animals do. Not to spoil it but to keep it groomed. Understanding the Earth and being a part of it, as the trees are a part of the Earth. When a tree grows that is when it has its voice.

Ricardo: What does it mean to be part of the Earth?

Karmu: To be one with the Earth.

Ricardo: Speak to us about peace, is peace among nations possible? Is world peace a possibility?

Karmu: Not as long as you have governments that stress individual grandeur and winner takes all. That breeds jealousy and endless trouble.

Ricardo: Well, the American government stresses individualism.

Karmu: It doesn't work. It causes the people to hate each other.

Ricardo: It pits one against another.

Karmu: Exactly, it doesn't work. It's better to have a social form of government where everybody helps everybody. If your boat is out of order everyone pitches in to help you repair it. It makes you feel good.

Ricardo: So you're talking about a place like Mexico.

Karmu: That's right. The black man who just ran for mayor of Boston lost the race because he pointed out that Fidel Castro does more good in the world than Ronald Reagan.

Ricardo: So you would say that Mel King's praise of Castro had a negative impact on his candidacy?

Karmu: Definitely.

Ricardo: What were some other factors accounting for Mel King not showing as well as he thought he would?

Karmu: Well black people figured it would be a wasted vote; they don't believe in themselves. Like the black Banner editor who spoke harshly against King. Well it's time for the black man to start loving himself and start appreciating his culture. He's got a rich heritage, he built pyramids.

Ricardo: How ancient Africans constructed pyramids is still a mystery.

Karmu: There are glyphs inside the pyramids of people flying saucer crafts.

Ricardo: Do you think these are beings from another place or are these Earthlings?

Karmu: These are Earthlings who had a skill and a wisdom that has been lost.

Ricardo: Let's move to the matter of nuclear holocaust. Do you think nuclear holocaust is possible?

Karmu: Very possible.

Ricardo: How can we avert that?

Karmu: By taking the men who have gone mad out of office. The men who are so obsessed by their own power that they think we can afford to lose five million people in a limited nuclear war.

Ricardo: The way to avert it is through the political process.

Karmu: Yes, getting them out of power is for the good of the people.

Ricardo: Change the power structure?

Karmu: Exactly.

Ricardo: How do we keep people in positions of power from becoming corrupted by their power?

Karmu: We need a governing board to keep those in power humane.

Ricardo: Could you say a little more about how we keep politicians humane?

Karmu: A coordinating board would only give the politicians a certain amount of money.

Ricardo: A ceiling on income level?

Karmu: It's a crime to give one man more money than he can spend.

Ricardo: I would like to speak to you about the Karmu Foundation. What is the present status of the foundation?

Karmu: It's lying in limbo with not too much happening. It's being talked about and people who want to support my healing work financially can do so, the way people support David Winfield's work with children.

Ricardo: What is a foundation?

Karmu: A foundation is a group of people who form with the aim of doing something for the public good in areas like education and health.

Ricardo: What is your vision associated with the establishment of a foundation?

Karmu: My vision is to get established in such a way that we're able to get funds to help young people become proud of who they are, so they can be of help to themselves, their people, and their government.

Ricardo: What do you plan to leave behind as a lasting testament to your work?

Karmu: I intend to leave the medications I've used, like the herbs. I will leave my teachings of how to use the medications, and my teachings about diet. Additionally, there will be teachings about the problems associated with lying and hating, as well as my teachings on moderation.

Ricardo: Many have asked about what your donations are used for. Clearly you do not swim in luxury, but I've heard some say 'what does his income go towards.' How do you respond to these inquiries about the aims towards which your funds are directed?

Karmu: They're directed towards staying alive and helping other people stay alive. Keeping down illness and disease is important. Right now I know a man trying to get five million to fight cancer. I need money in a similar way to instruct people, in simple ways, on how to take care of themselves naturally through nature's way.

Ricardo: Is the foundation being developed in any way?

Karmu: It's being discussed right now. We're getting people together who want to do something about it. We need personal help, funds are needed as well.

Ricardo: So is that how people who value your work contribute?

Karmu: If they want to help, keep it going. For example, I was on a boat where there was an outbreak of a skin fungus and people couldn't keep their food down. We gave them all of the solutions I made up for them to wash their clothes in, wash their dishes in, and drink. In a short time the disease outbreak was gone.

Ricardo: So if people wanted to be a part of this work they could contribute their time, energy, and funds, is that correct?

Karmu: That is correct.

Ricardo: What is the relationship between your Church and your goals for a foundation?

Karmu: The same ideals, but they are separate because you can conduct a Church on a small scale. You take individuals who are sick and pray for them, and get them to pray for each other. You also teach them the skills for using herbs properly, proper exercise, and proper diet. From that they can improve themselves.

Ricardo: What programs do you see your foundation carrying out?

Karmu: Self-help and helping each other. A self-help center is where when you come broke, hungry and cold, funds are set up for you, and you're assigned a place to live and work. If later on you want to start a business you're loaned money at no interest.

Ricardo: This would be the function of the foundation?

Karmu: That's right, to help people help themselves.

03 03 03

05

MISSION, SPIRITUALITY, MALADIES AND MEXICO

KARMU REFERRED to his center as a church. In this brief interview, he explains his concept of religion and its relationship to his work as a healer.

ON MISSION AND SPIRITUALITY

Ricardo: What is your mission in life?

Karmu: Our mission in life is to improve the lot of mankind. The mission involves handling problems that cross people's path and to improve them spiritually. Additionally, the mission is to improve mankind's health habits and their way of life.

Ricardo: How is the church related to your healing work? I know you have answered this to some extent.

Karmu: The church is a spiritual house where it is easier to bring out the God force in man for healing purposes.

Ricardo: Emanuel Swedenborg said there are two essentials of the church: The acknowledgment of the holiness of the word and the life of charity. What do you think of that, Karmu?

Karmu: I think it is normal and natural. God is in all of us and if we have knowledge of him we can call on God at any given time and get an answer. If you believe you are one with God, then that is the way it is.

Ricardo: Do you see your church as being in the Christian tradition?

Karmu: The church is in a spiritual tradition, which can be of any religion. Religion is something that man uses to call upon a higher being for help. A higher being within the self, which is God, it does not matter what religion or what type of religion; it all has the same purpose. The elevation of mankind through calling his inner spiritual essence is an activation of the sleeping God within.

Ricardo: If you were in my place as the interviewer, what question would ask about the Church of Karmu?

Karmu: The questions have been pretty well asked. The purpose of the church is to improve one's lot in life by calling upon the divinity, the spiritual higher being, to elevate one to a better place.

Ricardo: Thanks Karmu.

03 03 03

ON RACISM

True healers are generally wounded individuals. They come out of their great pain with the knowledge and ability to show others the way through. This was a subject that Karmu almost never spoke to directly, but in many ways he always spoke to it indirectly. It's very possible that his deepest wounds came about as a result of the invisibility hosted on him by American society.

In this interview Karmu addresses his attitudes towards race in America and the pain he experienced associated with racism.

Ricardo: How do you see the condition of Black people in America today?

Karmu: They are led around. They have what you call "token offerings." A few Blacks are working the better jobs, and when they work there long enough they are cast out. They generally are going on what you call a backward run.

Ricardo: Is racism still widespread in America?

Karmu: Definitely, you have people who are told by their fathers and mothers that people in other races are not like us. They are not the same as us. They are a different color and a different religion and they can't hope to compete with us. That's the general size of it.

Ricardo: Why does racism exist in this country?

Karmu: It exists because the Blacks were brought here and enslaved. The white man believed that Blacks were inferior to him. The white man spoke, the Black man jumped. He used Black women for sex. The Black man worked from dark to dark. A white man was considered in ill grace if he taught a Black man to read and write. The fact that Black people underwent these hardships made them strong. When you deprive a person he becomes stronger. Struggling makes him sharper. The best fighter is a hungry fighter. The Black man is hungry, therefore, he is a better fighter, he is a survivor – they made him a survivor.

Ricardo: What do you think Black people can do to improve their condition in America?

Karmu: They have to stick together, pick the right politicians who have promise and have proven they can do something and put them in office; no nonsense, no foolishness. If they prove they can help, put them in. There are enough Black people that if they vote in the same way they will effect change.

Ricardo: How has America benefited by the presence of Black people?

Karmu: He aided the culture and strengthened their breed by mingling the blood. There are hidden Blacks, whites with black ancestors, who have aided the white man's culture. Twenty-five percent of the inventions in this country were by Blacks. Eight of your American presidents were hidden Blacks. Many of your greatest heroes were Black, like Matthew Henson, the Black man who discovered the North Pole. The best athletes are Black; need I say more, black people contribute.

Ricardo: What do you see as the major problem facing this country?

Karmu: The major problem facing this country is how to give the country back to the people. It is ruled by politicians who have one thing in mind, their ego – the fact that they are white, the fact that they are the ruling class. The fact that they control the purse strings inflates their ego and they overlook other people. That's the reason why their airplanes don't fly and their ships sink in the ocean and they're being out-produced by the Japanese, Russians, Germans, and the Czechoslovakians. They'll be a third-rate country if they don't improve.

Ricardo: Will Blacks play a role in solving the problems?

Karmu: Definitely! There's no question about it. They're forging a way to the front. They're learning to take care of themselves. They want to take part in government. They want to know what's going on. This is our country too, and the problems are our problems. Let us learn about it so we can take the necessary steps to help solve the problems.

Ricardo: Will the United States maintain its prominence in the world today?

Karmu: I don't think so. The Germans and Japanese are out-producing them, out-maneuvering them, beating them by billions of dollars. The Japanese are exporting more than they are importing. Anytime a country gives you more than they take in, that demonstrates that they have the edge.

Ricardo: How did the United States lose its stronghold?

Karmu: By believing in white supremacy and by exploiting people. It's similar to the fall of the Roman Empire. Those in power become weak. They take to alcohol and orgies. The fall of the American Empire parallels the fall of the Roman and Greek Empire. The people become weak through success and stop working.

ଔ ଔ ଔ

ON MALADIES

I interviewed Karmu about his approach to treating some of the major illnesses in America such as Cancer and AIDS in March of 1984.

Ricardo: Do you treat individuals for cancer often?

Karmu: Quite often.

Ricardo: Can you give me some idea of the number of people that you have worked with?

Karmu: About a thousand.

Ricardo: That is a lot of people can you tell me about the treatments?

Karmu: You have to penetrate their subconscious and condition the mind. Let them know there is an unlimited higher power that will help them.

Ricardo: Are you saying you have been able to inspire hope?

Karmu: Well, you also have to cleanse the body and free up the energy centers. Free up the mind, the brain, the back, and the coccyx at the base of the spine, the legs and feet, the whole body. Then you have them take herbal baths to further heal them. Then put them on the proper herbal products, and put them on a special diet – a cleansing diet featuring garlic, onions, spinach, and other similar healing foods. We can heal them in this way, sometimes in as few as two visits. I healed one cancer patient that the hospital sent home to die. We had him pray, had his wife pray for him, had his neighbors pray for him, we cleansed him, and put him on a nutritious diet. We hit all the bases. The man is well now.

Ricardo: Can you tell me about another successful case?

Karmu: There was a school teacher who had a mastectomy, and came to me very depressed and in terrible condition due to constant pain. I got her taking daily baths in an herbal cleansing solution and I got her to stop drinking alcohol and smoking. We purged her system, got her reading the Holy Bible, and got her to exercise daily. She's happy now, she found relief.

Ricardo: What are some of the causes of cancer?

Karmu: Some of the contributing factors are stress, lack of money, uncertainty, job insecurity, toxic chemicals, and pollution in the air.

Ricardo: Are there certain people who are predisposed to developing cancer?

Karmu: Yes, people who worry a lot, people who are neurotic, and people who don't work enough with their hands. People who work with their hands tend to be more happy-go-lucky. These people tend not to get cancer. People with lots of stress and things like domestic problems run into these problems. People who have lots of time on their hands, people who worry a lot and don't exercise are the ones who get cancer.

Ricardo: Are their certain lifestyles that lead to people becoming more vulnerable?

Karmu: Yes, people who don't take care of themselves and people with nerve raking jobs, like bank presidents, airline pilots, and professors with too much responsibility. Students who don't get enough rest, or those who see their life as a failure because they can't get a good job.

Ricardo: What can be done to prevent this illness?

Karmu: I would suggest seeing a therapist to help solve your problems. It's important to feel good. Exercise, laughter, proper nutrition and prayer are all good ways to prevent this problem.

Ricardo: How about treating AIDS, have you treated AIDS?

Karmu: Once you become sexually active the body acquires a certain amount of disease. If the body gets weakened by such things as drug use and the body isn't cleansed, the germs in the body can cause the immune system to break down. Some people are what we call known carriers. Treating it is pretty much like treating cancer, you condition the mind, cleanse the body, and give them exercises to do.

Ricardo: How about treating herpes virus?

Karmu: We haven't been able to cure it, but we've been able to stop re-occurrences. Through medications and cleansing the system we can keep it in check. Stress can trigger it.

Ricardo: What's the best way to prevent it?

Karmu: Make sure your partner has been checked – good hygiene is important.

Ricardo: Can you say a little about diabetes?

Karmu: Diabetes is generally something you inherit, but in some cases eating too much sugar can play a part in causing it. Too much sugar and the wrong diet can throw the body out of balance. You treat it with insulin and proper nutrition. Lower your sugars and carbohydrates and eat healthy foods such as onion, garlic, and grains.

Ricardo: What causes arthritis?

Karmu: Well, you might inherit it or you could acquire it. People who work jobs where they experience a lot of contrast in weather are disposing themselves to it – like people who work under water.

Ricardo: How do you treat it?

Karmu: Here again the right exercise, proper herbs, the right diet and a person can be fine.

Ricardo: Could you talk a little about another one of your famous cases?

Karmu: We have a case right now of a woman about 20 years old who would get so tired she could barely even walk up a flight of stairs. We worked on her charkas and freed up her whole system. Now she is working full time again and saving her money. Her frame of mind has changed. If she keeps up with her exercises and eats the proper foods, I believe she will continue to be just fine.

Ricardo: It sounds like your treatment is pretty much always the same?

Karmu: The treatment depends on the individual, what ailment they have and how far the disease has advanced. For example, in advanced forms of cancer we might not be able to do anything about it. You have to remember most people have germs in their systems that can cause these various illnesses, but it's kept under control as long as they stay healthy. When under a lot of stress those germs can become a problem.

Ricardo: That's probably enough right there, thanks Karmu.

C03   C03   C03

VISIT TO MEXICO

Karmu rarely travelled far from home. When he returned from a trip to Mexico he seemed elated. The Mexican people he interacted with understood his role as a healer and treated him with reverence. This trip placed Karmu in his element.

Ricardo: Karmu, where did you go in Mexico?

Karmu: A place called Cancun.

Ricardo: What kind of accommodations?

Karmu: We stayed in a nice little house about 150 feet from the Ocean, which was accessible to tourists.

Ricardo: What kind of people did you encounter?

Karmu: We met a lot of tourists, but primarily we met Mayan Indians and Mexican people from all parts of Mexico. It's a new town and they are building it up. I met one man named Fernando who was building a 500-acre preserve for wildlife.

Ricardo: What similarities did you notice between Mexican people and American people?

Karmu: Mexican people are much kinder. They take you into their homes and exercise hospitality. They make you feel like one of them.

Ricardo: So, you like the Mexicans very much?

Karmu: The Mexican people set you on a pedestal, especially healers.

Ricardo: What kinds of ailments did you encounter while working with the people?

Karmu: Most of them had trouble with their teeth from drinking Coca-Cola and improper diet. There are a lot of proteins they don't get enough of and they drink too much beer. They have the known ailments like diabetes, heart troubles, and stress related disorders. The big problems stem from improper diet, improper dental care and stress.

Ricardo: What do their diet consist of?

Karmu: Their diet consists of tortillas, beans, mangoes, coconuts, greens; they eat tomatoes and lot of fruit, a lot of their diet revolves around beans.

Ricardo: Are the ailments you encountered there different from those Americans have?

Karmu: Yes, they don't have as much heart troubles. Most of the people lead a simple life. Things don't bother them too much.

Ricardo: How do they relax?

Karmu: They take time off during the day and sit in the sun or read the newspaper or sew.

Ricardo: And for a good time?

Karmu: Oh, everybody knows each other and they gather together to play and dance.

Ricardo: It really sounds like you were well received there.

Karmu: Oh yeah, best time in my life.

Ricardo: So you would consider going back there? Living there?

Karmu: I'm considering going back, but I don't know about living there. I think there may be a revolution there.

Ricardo: Are you talking about a change in government?

Karmu: Yes, the present government is corrupt and is creating too much friction.

Ricardo: So this is one of the things you learned while in Mexico?

Karmu: I learned that the air is clean, that the water is alright, that people get up early and work hard. Also, a lot of people live by fishing and that things are fairly inexpensive.

Ricardo: Did you experience any racism?

Karmu: None whatsoever. In fact when someone asked me questions they were all in Spanish and they were amazed when

I answered back in English.

Ricardo: Why do you think you didn't have to deal with racism?

Karmu: Because the Mexicans control their own destiny. They don't like the Americans. They don't like so-called gringos until gringos prove they can treat Mexicans fairly. In fact, they are suspicious of all gringos because they have been treated very badly by gringos in the past.

Ricardo: Is there any way in which Mexican culture is superior to American culture?

Karmu: Well, it teaches you to take care of your family. Families are very close, and you respect the elder people; you learn to revere them for their advice, wisdom and knowledge.

Ricardo: Is there any way in which American culture is superior to Mexican culture? What do we have over them culturally?

Karmu: Well, we use to have superior education, but I question if that's true now. They've got hundreds of Cuban teachers, directors, doctors, and so on, that are teaching the Mexican people to take care of themselves. They're doing a great job.

Ricardo: I think most Americans would look at that as communist influence.

Karmu: They call it a socialist government.

Ricardo: Is it a more equitable form of government?

Karmu: That's right.

Ricardo: What did you learn about Mexican lore, myth, tradition, history and things like that?

Karmu: I would say their friendliness. They are very, very friendly. They take time out to talk with you and make you feel loved. Everyone isn't in a big hurry.

Ricardo: Did you have any special experiences?

Karmu: The women next door would bring us fish. The man downstairs would bring us coconuts. The man with the fishing boat wanted to take me out on his boat. They made me feel loved and wanted – open doors and open hands. They kissed me on the cheek.

Ricardo: Why do you think it is that in general Americans know so little about Mexicans?

Karmu: One, because they're not taught. Two, because the media portrays Mexicans as illiterate people who have no common sense; backward people who take three-hour siestas and don't do anything.

Ricardo: Did you see yourself as having a special mission?

Karmu: I thought I could renew their way of healing. They had a name for me that means ancient healer. One who deals with roots and heals with faith and the laying-on-of-hands.

Ricardo: Curandero?

Karmu: That's the word.

Ricardo: Do you see yourself as having achieved that mission?

Karmu: Oh, definitely. There are Mexicans coming here to continue learning healing, especially some of the well-to-do ones, and if I go back there I'll be teaching.

Ricardo: Any other special insights that you gained?

Karmu: They don't worry too much about religion. The church has failed them as far as they are concerned and they have given up on religion.

Ricardo: That's very interesting. I tend to think of Mexicans as very religious, very Catholic as a matter of fact.

Karmu: They have given up on the Catholic religion. Where I was they didn't go to church on Sunday. They would go fishing instead.

Ricardo: Would you say that there is another religion developing among those people or are they letting that aspect go?

Karmu: They were brought up on the Catholic religion and the religion betrayed them as far as I can see. It didn't do anything for them.

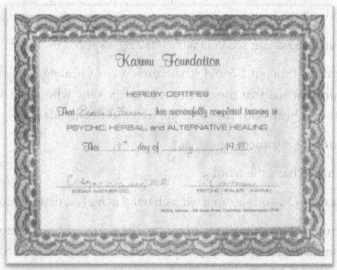

Karmu Foundation "Psychic, Herbal and Alternative Healing" Course Certificate of the author Dr. Ricardo Frazer

છ છ છ

06

KARMU SPEAKS ON JOE OTERI SHOW

DANNY SCHECTER and his associate producer Vicky Gregorian learned about Karmu and decided to bring him to speak on WLVI Television Channel 56. Karmu attended The Joe Oteri Show with one of his students, Compton O'Shaugnessy. Karmu provided intimate conversation that addressed a myriad of topics.

Joe: Can you be cured of a disease by the laying on of hands? What is psychic healing? Here to tell us about it is a man known as Karmu who says he is a psychic healer who's cured thousands of people. With him is Compton O'Shaugnessy. What's a psychic healer? What do you do?

Karmu: Laying on of hands operates through prayer. We penetrate the subconscious and get in tuned with the person who is ailing.

Joe: Now you say you lay on hands, you pray, and you get in tuned with them. Are you basically saying that you can cure psychosomatic illness, but not real physical illness?

Karmu: We heal all ailments known to man.

Joe: All ailments, so it's more than just getting in tuned with the person, it's not just psychosomatic people you cure.

Karmu: That's right.

Joe: If I have a broken leg, the bone is sticking out one way and I'm lying there in agony can you lay your hand on me and cure my broken leg?

Karmu: We had a woman with a broken ankle, it had been so for a long time. We prayed for her, laid on hands, and penetrated her subconscious. We now have it written in my book that she walked six miles and danced all night the next day.

Joe: The next day! Had she been in a cast? Was she being treated by the standard physicians?

Karmu: For several weeks.

Joe: And she took the cast off and went dancing and walking the next day.

Karmu: That's right.

Joe: Did they later take x-rays to see if the bone had in fact healed?

Karmu: They did.

Joe: And it had?

Karmu: It had been healed.

Joe: That's pretty interesting. What kind of techniques do you use other than the laying on of hands, I know from looking at your book there are certain things you do. Why don't you tell the audience about them?

Karmu: We use diet, exercise, and herbal preparations.

Joe: You mean if I have a poison in my system you could use a poultice of herb.

Karmu: We have a clay poultice with herbs that could take care of it.

Joe: That takes care of it, so it's more than just psychic healing you use. Besides the power of the mind, and prayer, you use natural substances like herbs and the rest of it.

Karmu: Natural substances, that's correct.

Joe: So it's not just psychic healing, it's a whole range of things.

Karmu: That's right.

Joe: Compton you're a student of Karmu, what did you learn?

Compton: Well the most important thing I learned was to have a very positive attitude about what could happen and what I did in fact see happening in Karmu's house.

Joe: What did you see?

Compton: I saw people come in who were very depressed. You talked first about emotional problems or psychosomatic illness, and a lot of people throughout the country are coming to realize that you can't really separate the physical and the emotional, there has to be a more holistic attitude towards health. At Karmu's house the whole person is treated. Yes there's psychic healing that goes on, and like your question about if you had a broken leg, I would advise you to go to the hospital and get it set because that is something that modern medicine can deal with and can deal with very accurately.

Joe: Adequately.

Compton: Yes.

Joe: Well, you see the thing that I'm fascinated by is I believe that a lot of the illnesses that we suffer from, particularly in a high powered society like America are psychosomatic, there in your mind, they don't really exist, but they're very painful to you. I can understand how your kind of treatment would help those people, but I have trouble bridging the gap with actual physical ailments, like the broken bone analogy.

Compton: Okay, I don't think the broken bone analogy is very good because that is something that can be so easily dealt with by standard medicine, but let's take a case of a person who has a disease like my mother had that could not be dealt with.

Joe: What did your mother have?

Compton: She was diagnosed as having multiple sclerosis. She was in the hospital; the left side of her body was becoming paralyzed. It eventually became totally paralyzed within the space of three days, and I went to the hospital, and I saw her there, and I asked how she was being treated, and there was no treatment. There is no treatment for this disease, and they weren't doing anything for her, and I didn't know what do, and I let my intuition take over and I said I've got to get her out of here. I brought her to my house and by using a combination of as Karmu says first aligning myself with her, allowing myself to you might say vibrate with her, laying on my hands, massaging her, loving her, hoping, praying for her that she would get well. I actually felt a negativity leave her body, and I knew at that exact moment it had happened, and I got her into bed. The next morning, I woke up to hear my mother in the front room walking and talking like normal and she hadn't been able to walk the day before.

Joe: That's amazing. Have you had any success treating people with cancer Karmu?

Karmu: Ninety percent.

Joe: Ninety percent cured!

Karmu: People from all over the world.

Joe: How do you know? Do you have any medical back-up?

Karmu: We do.

Joe: Really, what kind?

Karmu: Right now I'm working on a doctor from the Beth Israel Hospital in Brookline. He's diagnosed as having leukemia. After three visits I would say he's ninety percent healed.

Joe: You would say, but what does the medical profession say?

Karmu: They're about to take x-rays and confirm it.

Joe: Now, what kind of techniques, can you show the audience the techniques you use?

Karmu: Well, one technique would be to do the nerve centers, like so. This would be the third eye, a chakra. Free up all the nerve centers and give her the will. You penetrate her subconscious with your mind, I'm an agent, I take the energy from the cosmic arena, penetrate her subconscious with it, and she heals herself.

Joe: Where do your powers come from? Do you feel you've been selected by God? Do you see yourself as having special powers because I sure don't have that power? If I did that to her she'd punch me.

Karmu: I've got eight of my students healing cancer, all around the world.

Joe: You haven't answered my question, do you feel that God has singled you out.

Karmu: Definitely.

Joe: Now, you've told an interviewer that you walked on water?

Karmu: Yes, at nine years of age.

Joe: You actually walked across the swimming pool, or whatever.

Karmu: No, I fell off a raft with a raincoat and rubber boots on. I couldn't swim.

Joe: And you walked across?

Karmu: Yes.

Joe: How far did you walk?

Karmu: Oh, I would say about ten yards.

Joe: As a result of that did you become aware of your special significance?

Karmu: I was born with it. I healed by my presence at three months of age.

Joe: By your presence?

Karmu: That's right. If you're sick and sit in front of me, you'll get better.

Joe: And that is backed up by medical science? Now, I don't want to be blasphemous, but the only other person I've read about who had this kind of thing was a man named Jesus.

Karmu: Read page 5 or 8 of my book.

Compton: Well there is a testimonial about Karmu. Okay, Jesus was a person who transmitted healing energy. Also, to answer your question about selection, each individual has a talent they can do best. Now healing is definitely a talent, but everyone has the potential to be able to heal. What is happening when a mother puts her hand on the forehead of a child who is sick? She is in a way intuitively transmitting energy into that child and there are people who can learn to recognize the power in themselves, and learn how to develop it. Karmu happens to have been born with a great amount of vitality and what we call radiant white light that projects out to other people.

Joe: One thing I want you to answer for me, you also offer a number of services including cosmic cooking, flying lessons, and mating? Doesn't this somewhat demean your status as a chosen of God and a healer?

Karmu: It depends on how you take it. You need the proper foods to promote good health. We have herbal food, we show you how to make them up.

Joe: I see, thank you very much.

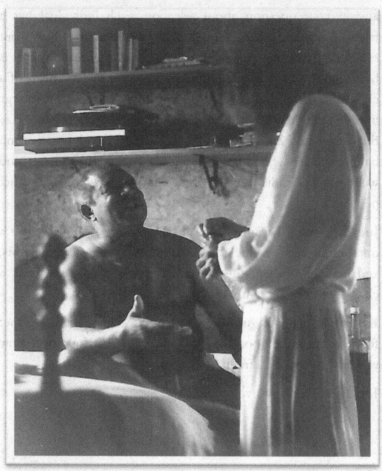

Karmu with a visitor – Photo by Dr. Ricardo Frazer

ભ ભ ભ

07

Karmu at Boston University School of Medicine

KARMU ADDRESSED the audience saying: We're here to discuss faith healing and healing with herbs. We use four methods. We use acupuncture, we use hypnosis, we use music therapy, and we invade the subconscious. We get very good results. It doesn't matter what they have, we have about a 97 percent success rate. We give herbs which purge the system and then we give massage. Sometimes the person is healed in five minutes, sometimes three months.

We just had a case about two weeks ago where a lady had cancer of the fallopian tube and she was supposed to have a hysterectomy. We gave her twenty hours of therapy and she never had the operation.

If there are any questions, I'll be glad to answer them. Questions about the methods we use: when, why, and what for.

Questioner: Could you talk about herbs?

Karmu: Yes, we use a number of herbs from Africa and the West Indies. I'll name some; we use bitter aloes, we use golden seal, we use garfield tea, we use root of the cassava weed, and a number of others.

Questioner: Can they be grown locally?

Karmu: Yes, they can be grown here. In fact, I've grown some in my backyard in Alston.

Questioner: Are these all for purging?

Karmu: No, they have various uses and effects. The bitter aloes and the goldenseal are used for purging; some are used for cooling off the blood, or raising the energy level. We have a combination that takes your energy right up. Capsules of goldenseal and aloes combined with the manipulation of certain acupuncture points will make you want to fly.

Questioner: Do you take any herbs regularly?

Karmu: Yes, I take them regularly myself. You never get sick, you never get tired and you feel good all the time.

Questioner: Same ones?

Karmu: Well we mix them up; it depends upon what's wrong with you. We do use a basic herbal preparation, but we also give certain ones depending upon what's wrong with you. If you blow your breath in your palm and you can't smell anything you're pretty clean inside.

Questioner: How did you learn all this?

Karmu: It has been in the family for generations and past down. My father was an Ethiopian Jew; my mother was Chinese and Black, and this and that. They were witchdoctors so it came naturally.

Questioner: Do you offer classes for the use of herbs?

Karmu: Oh yes, we have classes. A woman was in a coma in a hospital in New York and I worked on one of my disciples who in turn went to New York and touched the woman and she came out of the coma.

Questioner: Just touched her!

Karmu: Well, she massaged her nerve centers – like acupuncture, only it's called acupressure.

Questioner: Not bad.

Karmu: No, I'd be glad to teach anyone who wants to learn.

Questioner: Could you give sort of a mini lesson?

Karmu: Right here?

Questioner: Sure.

Karmu: Step over, I'd be glad to. Okay, sit down here and turn your back towards me. We do a thing like this, we take the nerve centers and we activate them. When I get through you won't know it's you. Next time you take an examination come to me first and I'll make sure you pass it. How do you feel?

Questioner: I'm not sure what I went through.

Karmu: How do you feel anyway?

Questioner: Very light headed.

Karmu: Now your mind is very active, and you have a sense of wellness.

Questioner: It feels good. I should get that every morning.

Karmu: You see we have activated the nerve centers and we've giving the body balance. Stimulating the nerve centers this way creates what we call free mental association and balance. Everything works in unison like a finely coached ball-team.

Karmu gives you a place in the sun – Photo by Dr. Ricardo Frazer

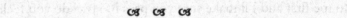

08

BLUE MEDICINE AND COSMIC ENERGY

I CONTINUE the question and answer format as Karmu shares one of his wellness tonics and concept of cosmic energy. As with many conversations with Karmu, I felt like conversations at times were going in one direction, but it ended up totally somewhere else. When I visited Karmu again he was on his bed, on his back, doing exercises.

Karmu: I work out every day. I do special exercises that I devised so you can exercise right in bed. I want you to learn them. This one is good for the stomach, abdomen, and the low back. Lift your butt off the bed. Circle to the right five times, then circle to the left five times. Repeat that process five times. Make sure you get a good rhythm going with your breathing – deep breathing from the stomach.

Ricardo: That looks pretty erotic, Karmu.

Karmu: Never mind that, it works. I've been doing these exercises my whole life. I'm as strong as an ox with great body tone. At 72 I'm still going strong. I last longer than most men. You need to do the one I just showed you. I recommend that you have a medical doctor check out your stomach. You've got something going on there. I'd also suggest that you get some colonics.

Ricardo: What's a colonic, Karmu? I've never hear of that.

Karmu: It's a special kind of deep enema. Most disease starts in your colon. You can get a colonic at Ann Wigmore's center across the river in Boston. They'll turn you on to wheat grass too. I don't use it but a lot of my patients have gotten great results with it and swear by it.

Ricardo: What's blue medicine all about, Karmu, I'd like to learn more about it.

Karmu: It's chemical, potassium. It was used regularly in hospitals to disinfect surgical tools. Then the government had it taken off the market. I've heard it can be used to make explosives. That's how things work in this country. If it's cheap, readily available and effective the medical establishment will use the government to get rid of it. It's all about making money in this country.

At that point a very attractive middle age women knocked on the kitchen door and came into the bedroom. I really need your help Karmu, she seemed a bit frantic.

Karmu: Where have you been movie star? Didn't I tell you to come around more often? You look really, really good. I should take you for myself. You were made for love. I rest my case. Golden boy, go up to corner and get me a quart of that high-grade brandy. I need it for my medicine.

Karmu located a few dollars and handed it to me. I suspected he was trying to get rid of me for a while. I was happy to do the errand. Karmu was real generous with me so any opportunity to assist him felt like a blessing.

When I returned I learned that the women was married to a member of the mafia and that she had run away. She felt trapped and abused in the relationship, so she left but she was real scared and didn't know what to do.

Apparently, Karmu had interactions with her husband

Flower children came too – Art by Dr. Ricardo Frazer

and knew about his involvement with the mob. While I was gone, Karmu had managed to calm her down and alleviate some of her fears. I don't know what he did or what he said to her. Karmu seemed totally fearless. But a few other people walked in while she was there and since I was just hanging around she and I began to talk.

I found out that she was scared for her life and felt that she had to return to her husband. She told me that she had gotten with her husband when she was very young and it took quite some time before she really knew what he did for a living. She felt there was nowhere she could go without being tracked down. So she was just going to wait it out for a while and then return home. I felt sorry for her. I got the impression she valued having someone to talk to, so that's what I did, I talked with her. I thought she was very attractive. Her hair was recently done, she was well manicured and she wore a mink coat. I got the impression that she had a comfortable life, materially, but didn't want that life anymore because she lived in fear.

I started visiting Karmu about two times a week over the course of the next four or five years. At some point I suggested to him that I would like to write a book about him. He liked the idea and I began conducting structured interview with him and recording them on cassette tape, in order to transcribe them later.

 os   os   os

MY FIRST STRUCTURED INTERVIEW WITH KARMU

Ricardo: You've stated that you can cure all ailments; do you still feel that way?

Karmu: Provided the patient has an open mind. Some people have built-in prejudices. We had a case of a young man who was using shelves of medication the first time he came here. When he came back all his ailments had left. We gave him therapy and a short time later he came back and his ailments were gone. Therefore, we conclude the problem was in his mind. If a person has an open mind we can heal almost anything.

Ricardo: How would you heal a person that had arthritis?

Karmu: We would immerse him in blue solution. Then we would manipulate his energy centers and talk to him in a positive manner; become him; talk to him in his own language. Therefore, you reach the mind and you reach the body.

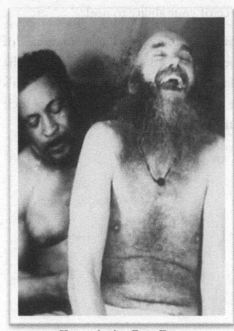

Karmu healing Ram Dass
Photo by R.J. Levison

Ricardo: How would you heal an adult that had back pains?

Karmu: There again you would penetrate the subconscious and free up the energy centers. Check his diet and see what he is taking wrong; give him the proper foods. Teach his friends to manipulate his energy centers, the coccyx, up and down the spine, and the rest of the body. We generally can heal back pains this way. Freeing up the nerve/energy centers is a key. In fact a blocked energy center in the neck stops the energy from going through the body. The result is the body does not function at full capacity. To give a person health you have to open up all his energy centers. That means going over the whole body.

Ricardo: So generally the approach is the same regardless of the ailment. Is that true?

Karmu: Unless the person is in a coma. In that case you manipulate the energy centers of his head. Their subconscious can accept information from your conscious mind even when the person is in a coma.

Ricardo: What's the source of your ability to heal?

Karmu: A lot of energy and the ability to act as a conductor of energy; cosmic energy from space, plus an understanding of the human body and the ability to place myself inside the person's consciousness. I become them, feel their pain, take on their pain, and disperse it into the cosmic arena.

❧ ❧ ❧

09

KARMU'S APOTHECARY: MEDICAL USE OF HERBS

THE MEDICAL use of herbs has been of great interest to many natural health practitioners and scientific researchers. This chapter offers an introduction to some of the herbs and supplements Karmu used as remedies. Many often forget that plants have been the source of proficient medicines since ancient times. They are the foundation of modern medicines and are used for the treatment and cure of many diseases and skin problems.

Drugs used today were synthesized from and contain active ingredients derived from plants. Ancient doctors collected information about herbs and developed well-defined pharmacopoeias to treat many disorders. Karmu used herbs and other protocols to treat a host of medical conditions including AIDS, cancer, joint pain, hypertension, sleep disorders, hormonal irregularity, headaches, skin issues, and a host of other conditions.

Blue Medicine

Karmu perceived all of his patients to be in need of

detoxification because he believed that Americans received high levels of toxins through daily activity. His primary method of detoxification was potassium permanganate. This chemical can be obtained legally through chemical supply houses, and had been used for centuries for its germicidal proprieties.

Karmu recommended it for baths (a cup or two in a bathtub with two tablespoons of sudsy ammonia), enemas, gargle, foot soak, douche, and to wash the eyes, nose, and ears. Potassium permanganate can lead to poisoning and tissue damage if used at too high a concentration, so Karmu carefully supervised its use and administration. Karmu also believed that he could "charge" the crystals with his energy and usually only gave it out in solution.

Red Medicine

When Black Medicine was mixed with alcohol it was referred to as Red medicine. Red medicine was a mixture of fermented fruits and juices (sometimes he called it "red eye") used in social gatherings to lift the spirits and provide medicinal benefits. Karmu was extremely practical and used every opportunity to heal his patients.

Metal Objects

Karmu kept a box of metal objects close to him (often under his bed) to absorb his energy. These objects were given to selected individuals.

Karmu Hairs

Karmu also gave out pieces of his hair and instructed people to keep it with them, and to even hold it over "affected parts of the body" from time to time. Karmu was very much into the concept of energy and applied it everywhere.

Purification

Burning sulfur and salt was advocated to remove negative energies. Cloves and garlic were suggested for use over windows and doors to keep out negative energies. On occasion Karmu also recommended the burning of sage for the purification of negative energy, but he was concerned about burning it since he lived in an urban city and believed that its smell could cause it to be misconstrued as the burning of cannabis, which was an illegal, controlled substance.

KARMU'S HEALING HERBS AND THEIR APPLICATIONS

Black Medicine

Karmu referred to his primary herbal combination as black medicine. The precise formulae that he used is known to some individuals (I myself do not know it). The seven primary herbs Karmu used in his formula were: aloe, ginseng, golden seal, rosemary, sassafras, snakeroot, and valerian. Karmu recommended individual herbs, but usually administered them in the combination of seven herbs. The herbal information presented here was given to me by Karmu. *Back to Eden* by Jethro Kloss appears to have been the primary source for much of this information regarding herbs:

Aloe (aloe socotrina) is a cathartic, stomachic, aromatic, and emmenagogue. Leaves are used. Promotes menstruation. Will expel pinworms after several doses. This herb is used in many cathartics to help clean out the colon. To assist with moving the bowels, take: 1 oz. powdered buckthorn bark, 1 oz. powdered rhubarb root, 1 oz. powdered mandrake root, ¼ oz.

powdered aloe, and 1 oz. powdered calamus root. Start with ¼ tsp. of this mixture and adjust the dosage according to individual needs.

Aloe is one of the finest colon and body cleansers – cleanses morbid matter from the stomach, liver, kidneys, spleen, bladder and colon. It can be used in any case where a laxative is needed – does not gripe, and is very healing and soothing. Aloes may be used for any kind of external sores, and is an excellent remedy for piles and hemorrhoids. Add one heaping teaspoonful of powder to a pint of water and strain. Adding two tsp. of borac acid is beneficial and will help keep the mixture from becoming sour.

Ginseng (Pannax quinquefolia) is a demulcent, stomachic, and stimulant. Ginseng helps promote appetite, improved mood, energy and is useful in digestive disturbances. When flavored, makes an agreeable drink for colds, chest troubles, and coughs. Good for stomach troubles, constipation, lung troubles, and inflammation of the urinary tract.

Golden Seal (Hydrastis canadensis) is a laxative, tonic, alterative, detergent, opthalmicum, antiperiodic, aperients, diuretic, antiseptic, and deobstruent. It is one of the best substitutes for quinine. It is an excellent remedy for colds, grippe, stomach troubles, and liver troubles. It benefits mucous membranes and tissues that it comes in contact with. Good for open sores, inflammations, eczema, ringworm, erysipelas, or many skin diseases. Golden seal tea is made by steeping one teaspoonful in a pint of boiling water for 20 minutes. Can be used as a wash – clean the skin with hydrogen peroxide, sprinkle the powered root on the skin, and cover.

Taken in small but frequent doses, it will allay nausea during pregnancy. Steep a tsp. in a pint of boiling water for 20 minutes, stir well, let settle, and pour off the liquid. Take 6 tablespoons a day and it will improve circulation. Combined with skullcap and red cayenne pepper will greatly relieve and strengthen the heart. It has no superior when combined with myrrh (1 part golden seal to ¼ part myrrh) for ulcerated stomach, duodenum, and dyspepsia. It is especially good for enlarged tonsils and mouth sores. Smoker's sores (caused by holding a pipe in the mouth), will heal after a few applications of powder to the sores.

Golden seal combined with myrrh and cayenne is an excellent remedy for diphtheria, tonsillitis, and other throat troubles. Good for chronic catarrh of the intestines and all catarrhal conditions. Will improve appetite and aid digestion. Combined with skullcap and hops it makes an excellent tonic for spinal nerves, very good for spinal meningitis, skin eruptions, scarlet fever and smallpox.

To cure pyorrhea or sore gums, put some of the tea in a cup, dip toothbrush in solution, and thoroughly brush teeth and gums. For any nose trouble, pour some tea into the palm of the hand and snuff up the nose.

Golden seal is useful in typhoid fever, gonorrhea, leucorrhea and syphilis. For bladder troubles, have a nurse or physician inject golden seal solution into the bladder with a rubber catheter immediately after the bladder has been emptied, and retain as long as possible – repeating 2 or 3 times a day.

Two parts golden seal combined with one part wild alum, taken internally, is a laxative and excellent remedy for bowel and bladder troubles. Good for piles, hemorrhoids, and prostate gland. When combined with equal parts red clover blossoms, yellow dock, and dandelion it has a wonderful effect on the gall bladder, kidneys, liver, and pancreas. Combined with peach leaves, queen of the meadow, cleaver and corn silk, it is a reliable remedy for Bright's disease and diabetes.

It is an excellent remedy for the eyes if the eyelids are granulated or there is film over the eyes: steep a tsp. of golden seal and one of boric acid in a pint of boiling water, stir well, let cool, and pour off the liquid. Put a tablespoonful of this remedy in a half cup of water and bathe the eyes, using an eye dropper or eye cup. If used a little too strong, it will hurt a little, but there is no harm done.

Take ¼ tsp. of golden seal dissolved in a glass of hot water immediately on arising, and one hour before the noon and evening meals. Or, steep a teaspoon in a pint of boiling water, stir well, let cool, pour the liquid off and take a tablespoonful 4 to 6 times a day. Children should take less of all doses, according to age.

Chronic catarrh of the intestines can be helped with golden seal. Produces healing in ulceration of the mucous lining of the rectum and is effective in hemorrhage of the rectum. It is a remedy for chronic and intermittent malarial poisoning or enlarged spleen due to malaria.

Rosemary (rosemarinus officinalis) is a stimulant, antispasmodic, emmenagogue, tonic, astringent, diaphoretic, carminative, nerving, aromatic, and cephalic. Leaves and flower are used. Good for colds, colic, nervous conditions, and nervous headaches. Rosemary should be taken warm for these complaints. Good as wash for mouth, gums, bad breath and sore throat. The leaves are used for flavoring foods. Rosemary oil is used as a perfume for ointments and liniments. It is an excellent ingredient for shampoos. Rosemary aids digestion, coughs, consumption, mental imbalance, and strengthens eyes.

Sassafras (sassafras officianale) is aromatic, stimulant, alterative, diaphoretic, and diuretic. The bark of the root is used. Purifies blood and cleanses entire system. Good for flavoring herbs that have a disagreeable taste. Useful as a stomach and bowel tonic and relieves gas. Taken warm, sassafras is an excellent remedy for spasms. Sassafras is a useful treatment for colic, skin diseases and eruptions. Good wash for inflamed eyes. Sassafras is very good for kidneys, bladder, varicose ulcers, chest and throat troubles. Oil of sassafras is excellent for toothaches.

Snakeroot (aristolochia serpentaria) is a stimulant, tonic, and diaphoretic. Dried rhizomes and roots are used. In the United States, it is grown primarily in central and southern states. Small doses will promote appetite, and tone digestive organs. Too large a dose will produce nausea, and griping pains in bowels. Recommended for intermittent fevers – may be used as an adjunct to quinine. In strong doses produces increased arterial action, diaphoresis and diuresis.

Snakeroot excels in eruptive fever where the eruption is tardy, or in the typhoid stage where a strong stimulant cannot be used. Snakeroot helps to promote recovery in chronic forms of gouty inflammation. Excessive boiling impairs its virtues. A cold infusion is useful in convalescence from acute diseases. Dosage: powder root: 10 to 30 grains. Fluid extract: ½ to 1 drachm.

Valerian (valeriana officinal) is aromatic, stimulant, tonic, anodyne, antispasmodic, and nervine. Valerian is an excellent nerve tonic – very quieting and soothing. Promotes menstruation – taken hot. Valerian is excellent for children with measles, scarlet fever or restlessness – 2 tablespoons 2 or 3 times daily. Good for convulsions in infants and is useful for colic, low fevers, colds, and for gravel in the bladder. Heals an ulcerated stomach, prevents fermentation and gas. The tea is healing when applied to sores and pimples externally – must be taken internally at the same time. Valerian helps to relieve palpitation of the heart. Root should not be boiled.

 C8 C8 C8

10

HOLISTIC HEALTH PRACTICES

SWAMI MUKTANANDA Karmu (Edgar H. Warner) was born in August 1910. He said that when he was an infant, people who were ill would visit his parents' home and get to hold him because he could heal by his presence at birth. Karmu boldly shared that the people who held him were healed of all kinds of ailments. He learned about and practiced healing throughout his life, but moved fully into his great mission as a holistic healer and an agent for social change when he retired from his career as an auto mechanic.

His system was constructed on a foundation of traditional Asian and African healing. He embodied a brand of psychology that was comprehensive, integrative, and incorporated the best practices of modern psychology. He synthesized some of the best theoretical insights of modern psychology into a practice that he used to guide and help legions of individuals struggling to overcome and deal with the hardships of modern living.

This chapter is focused on my perspective regarding the tenets of his psychological approach. While examining his practice one finds ideas articulated by Sigmund Freud, Carl Jung, Alfred Adler, and other central figures in the history of scientific psychology, especially, Freud's psychoanalysis, Jung's analytical psychology and Adler's social interest.

Freud articulated a foundation for a scientific approach to understanding the unconscious mind. The unconscious was viewed as uncritical, programmable, and the reservoir of the individual's experiences. Dream interpretation was viewed as a way to access unconscious information. Insight was understood as a critical step towards changing unconscious programming. Hypnosis was viewed as a tool for enhancing individual recall of repressed and suppressed information, as well as a tool for changing existing programming, using suggestion.

Karmu employed all of these elements in his practice. He would let you know that he was penetrating your subconscious mind – I believe that he practiced a form of hypnosis in order to achieve this. One key to his hypnotic method was the way he modulated his speech patterns and tone. He spoke very fast, sometime very softly, and other times very slowly, in an intentional orchestration. He often by-passed the conscious mind and subliminally imported suggestions into the person's subconscious, in order to alter the client's beliefs.

If you didn't pay close attention, these techniques would go unnoticed. He understood the power of belief in changing the structure of an individual's reality. He would speak of mind boggling things such as his visitations to a person while they were dreaming (e.g., catching them as they fell from a high cliff). The patient's conscious mind would be transported to a place where he could speak directly to the divinity at the core of the individual's being.

When he spoke with conviction of things like his walking through walls, or walking on water, the conscious mind would be befuddled, but the spiritual nature of the person was encouraged to drop all sense perception of inherent limitation.

He understood that spirit is limitless. The spirit of each person was directed to soar beyond the boundaries of physical limitation – a reminder of our true essence as spirits living a material existence. He was a very fine hypnotist. Occasionally, he might even supplement these procedures with a few sips of an intoxicating, alcohol-based "red medicine." Red medicine was an herbal preparation that reduced inhibitions and seemed to facilitate the hypnotic induction.

Karmu was a highly intelligent person even though he lacked formal academic training at institutions of higher education. He understood human nature, American society, and the multi-dimensional forces operating on the individual. A person, who is open-minded, would grow in his insights about his self and the societal forces operating in his daily lives. These insights facilitate the growth of the individual ego.

In addition to treating the whole person and fostering a sense of purpose, mission in life, and individual goals, he directed each person to further develop innate potentials, to harness inherent abilities, and to effect change in the world. Each person was accepted and no one was rejected, regardless of station in life, life circumstances, or ability to pay.

He adapted himself to the needs of each person, and many of us were brought together to assist each other in our divine missions. He could see into each individual psyche and elevate their being, and their activity. He built up a person's self-esteem, and self-confidence and willed them to get better. He taught that each genuine spiritual tradition was valid and had the same ultimate goal of union with the divine. Spiritual and psychological growth was fostered through a merger of psychological and spiritual practice.

He used his highly developed compassion and finely tuned empathic skills to model how we should be in the world. He taught that we should be loving, kind, respectful, compassionate and giving – he exemplified this behavior. Spiritual development was fostered pragmatically through practice, as well as reflection and conversation. He gave freely without expectation of return, thus creating an ascending vortex for change with himself at the center. His energy still vibrates and resonates in those of us who could see his value, and the blessings to be obtained through contact and connection with him.

Karmu, like Alfred Adler, used individual psychology as agency in social change. He was deeply political and pressed you to better understand the political system, the political forces in play, and social history, especially as it applied to human oppression. He was deeply sensitive regarding man's inhumanity towards others, and deeply committed to articulating these issues, regardless of how he was perceived. There were no sacred cows when it came to his political opinions. He said it the way he saw it, and pressed you to develop your social self, your social interest, and to become an agent for social change in your daily interactions.

He understood, like Adler, that our long experience of dependency fostered an inferiority complex in each of us that was overcome through active social agency. As such, few healing sessions were complete without a lesson in current politics. He would call people out, and name names. No holds were barred, no villain unscathed, and certainly no blaming of the victim. He activated our moral compass and gave it direction.

Karmu's system of psychology was open, dynamic, and spiritual. It addressed body, mind, and soul. The conscious and unconscious minds were addressed as he helped people to develop towards cosmic consciousness. Our divine spark was ignited by a Karmu led journey into the cosmic arena. We became more conscious of who we already were – cosmic beings of love and light on a divine mission to change the world.

The Karmu system of physical health placed emphasis on diet, exercise, detoxification, the laying on of hands, and massage. His approach to detoxification was fairly consistent, regardless of the ailment he was treating. All of his patients were instructed to detoxify using a solution of potassium permanganate that he regulated. This chemical was said by Karmu to be charged with his energy and he determined the concentration of the solution. As a patient, you were expected to bathe in this blue solution and to do a warm water foot soak in the solution regularly.

Potassium permanganate is legal chemical that can be bought through chemical supply companies. It's a strong oxidizer that is flammable. This chemical should not be mixed in any higher concentration than one that has the color of dark amethyst (1/4 tsp. per quart of water). Doses of 10 grams or so (a very, very large dose compared to Karmu's Blue Medicine) can lead to poisoning, including fatal toxicity. Karmu regulated the dosage, keeping it at safe levels, and was highly adept in its use.

However, he is gone now, so those who use it medicinally should not use it as an eye bath since it is damaging to eye tissue and can cause severe burning. Ingestion is also a highly questionable practice, since it can cause severe burns to mucus membranes of the mouth, throat, esophagus, and stomach. When bathing in the solution, a cup or two with a couple tablespoons of sudsy ammonia is sufficient. When the water cools down it can be heated again and when the water changes color you have probably received the full benefit of the bath. For those concerned about the purple coloration that can result from this solution, hydrogen peroxide can also be used to neutralize the color.

Karmu placed diet at the core of health care; however, dietary recommendations were individually-based and tailored to the specific health concerns of each person. He stressed the eating of a balanced healthy diet including fruits, vegetables, proteins, grains and carbohydrates, however he stressed moderation in all things, and seemed to shun extreme diets. He also recommended an occasional fast or break from eating.

He also encouraged me to exercise as much as possible and taught me many exercises that he had developed for people who were confined to their bed. Massage was another real cornerstone in his protocol. He taught me his form of massage, using olive oil-based concoctions that he would put together and sometimes refer to as white medicine. He liked to assign colors to his medicines. For example, Black medicine was his general combination of herbs that would become Red medicine when brandy was added. I became quite skillful at giving massages, as a result of his training, and he also stress self-massage.

His approach was that of the deep-tissue variety that had to be done with a high degree of skill and sensitivity. His approach included hand and foot reflexology and required the development of bodily intuition. Tuning in to energy was always a focus of the training. Under his tutelage your hands became skilled in where to go and how much pressure to apply. A gentle tapping motion was his signature move. There was also a psychology underlying the massage that he taught since massage was expected to bring up emotional pain and psychological content. There were many psychological dynamics to massage that he passed on verbally. These teachings which involved a lot of discussion about human sexuality and the transmission of energy seemed to be at the core of his instruction.

He worked on the physical and psychological level, but he also worked on the spiritual. While he seemed careful to teach no particular religious tradition, he taught a great deal of spiritually and encouraged you to learn from all religions. He said that all religions had the same source and the same goal. He would direct me to pay attention to things that were seemingly insignificant, like the meaning of a bird landing on his window sill. He encouraged me to pay attention to the type of bird and to assign a meaning to the bird's appearance at that time – he didn't believe in coincidence or accidents.

He would also give you metal that had been in his presence for a period of time, or give you locks of his hair. These objects were said to have protective, energetic, and beneficial properties. He also believed in clearing negative energy, and recommended substances for this purpose such as the burning of sulfur and salt together, the burning of sage, or the use of garlic and cloves.

He taught that everyone could be psychic when they attended to it, practiced, and learned to shift their consciousness into relaxed, receptive states. Karmu had a very natural, down-to-earth, practical approach to healing. He made you feel that everyone could do what he did, that there was nothing supernatural about it. I myself decided that there were some things that I just didn't want to do – like take other people's pain and disease into my body. No thanks!

CB CB CB

11

PSYCHOLOGICAL WELLNESS PERSPECTIVES

KARMU WORKED on the body, the mind, and the soul because he was a holistic healer who believed that the integration of these spheres of human functioning influenced overall wellness. Many chapters of this book focus on the treatment of the body. The present chapter places emphasis on the mind and utilizes a biographical approach. Psychological wellness has become a central concept in positive psychology. The current state of affairs in psychological wellness theory and research suggest that it might benefit from developing a wider lens.

Important goals in the positive psychology subdivision of humanistic psychology include nurturing what is best in people and understanding psychological wellness. Positive psychology is a school of psychology that addresses what is right about people. This school represents an optimistic system of psychology that builds on the work of early humanistic psychologists such as Abraham Maslow and Carl Rogers.

The purpose of psychology from this optimistic perspective

is to help individuals actualize and to increase understanding of psychological wellness. The present investigation into psychological wellness integrates nomothetic and ideographic approaches and is based on biographical information about an individual who appeared to manifest psychological wellness at an optimal level. An ideographic phenomenological approach is merged with objective scientific investigation in this chapter.

A Theory of Wellness

Individual wholeness and self-actualization are major goals of humanistic psychology. Eastern spirituality has influenced positive psychology, although these trends tend to be more implicit than explicit. Psychological wellness has been defined as having a positive sense of meaning and purpose in life along with the perception that life outcomes will be positive. It has also been defined as a dynamic evolutionary process involving constant growth and adaptation.

There are many definitions of psychological wellness. Theory development and measurement of psychological wellness are ongoing since it is still unclear what psychological wellness means or how to measure it. A cogent and comprehensive theory of psychological wellness that gives coherence to the vast number of definitions and models is needed.

Psychological wellness is a highly complex, synergistic, and multi-dimensional construct. Optimal functioning occurs when the constituent dimensions of psychological wellness are in balance. Wellness theory development appears to be in the embryonic stage. Consequently, there are many definitions but no consensus regarding the components of psychological wellness. Generally speaking, the components identified have been grouped into "aspects of the self" or "aspects of domains in life". Possible aspects of the self that have been identified are self-actualization, locus of control, sense of coherence, and emotional intelligence.

Domains in life include emotional wellness, intellectual wellness, physical wellness, social wellness, spiritual wellness, occupational wellness, and environmental wellness. All dimensions are said to interact in a manner such that the whole is greater than the sum of the parts.

New Terrain for Psychological Wellness

Perception is a central element in psychological wellness. As such, the distinction between "psychological wellness" and "perceived psychological wellness" is important. Definitions of wellness tend to focus on areas of health or strength rather than on the absence of illness. Empirical data also indicates that perceptions are valid indicators of future objective health. Culture is an important determinant of psychological wellness; just as there are cultural determinants of perception, people perceive and experience reality through a cultural lens.

In the present chapter, the author surveyed different schools of psychology. Variables were identified that might be linked together in meaningful ways to extend what we currently know about psychological wellness. This chapter represents a trailblazing investigation rather than a compendium of existing theory and research. Although that information is incorporated, new terrain is explored.

Meta-Theoretical Development

Developing a meta-theory may be a valuable step towards understanding psychological wellness. Meta-theory has been defined as "The development of overarching combinations of theory, as well as the development and application of theorems for analysis that reveal underlying assumptions about theory and theorizing."

Psychological traditions considered include Jung's analytical psychology, Maslow's humanistic and transpersonal psychology, and Chopra's complementary medicine. Csikszentmihalyi's positive psychology, Myers' optimal psychology, and Cross' racial identity theory are also important. Adler's individual psychology, Bandura's social learning theory, and the Karmu System may also be of great benefit. These theories provide insights that contribute towards a more comprehensive theory of psychological wellness.

Exploration of these schools of thought suggests that self-realization/actualization, cultural identity, resiliency, social interest, and self-efficacy are aspects of the self that are also worthy of exploration as constituent dimensions of psychological wellness. The concepts of flow and trance may be domains in life worthy of integration into the psychological wellness construct.

Lastly, a holistic healer is presented as a model of psychological wellness. This "healer" was a living example of someone who embodied and incorporated a holistic approach, attaining psychological wellness at a high level of human functioning.

Karmu the Holistic Healer

An ideographic approach will be used to explore psychological wellness by investigating the work of a "holistic healer". Karmu was a well-known healer who provided a practical model for achieving health and wellness. He was a living, breathing example of a holistic way to understand and approach wellness, and he embodied what is possible when the mind, body, and spirit operate in harmony.

Edgar H. Warner (Karmu) was born in August 1910. He identified himself as a psychic healer and completed his great work as a healer and an agent for social change. He practiced a system of holistic healthcare based on traditional Asian and African healing methods and incorporated psychology into his approach. Karmu incorporated a brand of psychology that was comprehensive, integrative, and included many of the best practices in modern psychology. He helped legions of individuals struggling to overcome and deal with the hardships of modern living. Throughout his teaching and practice, one also finds ideas presented in the writings of Sigmund Freud, Carl Jung, Alfred Adler, and other prominent figures in the history of western psychology. Ultimately, Karmu's system was holistic and based on Kemetic philosophy.

Karmu practiced a form of hypnosis in order to affect the patient's subconscious mind and he could will the person to get better. He would tell his clients he was "penetrating their subconscious mind." One key to his hypnotic method was the way he modulated his speech patterns and tone. He intentionally orchestrated his speech and spoke very fast, sometimes very softly, and other times very slowly. He was able to by-pass the conscious mind and subliminally induce suggestions into the person's subconscious, in order to alter the client's beliefs.

He used a lot of positive reinforcement to strengthen the person's ego. Techniques such as these would go unnoticed if one did not pay close attention. He understood how to change the structure of an individual's reality. He would speak of mind-boggling things such as him walking on water at a young age and visitations with a person while they were dreaming (e.g., catching them as they fell from a high cliff). Karmu could transform a client's subconscious mind and he knew how to speak directly to the divinity at the core of an individual's being.

Karmu stated with conviction that he walked through walls and walked on water. This kind of discourse befuddles the conscious mind, but encourages us to drop all sensory perception of inherent limitation. Our soul is directed to soar beyond the boundaries of physical limitation. We are reminded that we are Spirit living a material existence. Karmu's unquestioning faith in the unlimited power of Spirit was infectious. He was also a skilled hypnotist who appeared to practice hypnosis effortlessly and naturally. Occasionally, he might even supplement these procedures with a few sips of an intoxicating alcohol-based "red medicine" – a medicinal herbal preparation that reduced inhibitions and may have facilitated the hypnotic induction.

He understood American society, human nature, and the multidimensional forces operating on the individual. Open-minded patient's insight into self and the societal forces operating in their daily lives grew. These insights facilitated the growth of the individual ego and the movement towards ego transcendence. He treated the whole person and fostered a sense of purpose, mission in life, and the achievement of individual goals. He directed each person to develop their innate potentials, to harness inherent abilities, and to affect change in the world. Each person was accepted and no one was rejected, regardless of station in life, life circumstances, or ability to pay. He adapted himself to the needs of each person and many of us were brought together to assist each other in our divine missions. He could see into each individual psyche and elevate that person. Karmu taught that each genuine spiritual tradition had validity and value and the same ultimate goal of union with the divine.

Spiritual and psychological growth was fostered through a merger of psychological and spiritual practice. He used compassion and finely tuned empathic skill to model how we should be in the world. He taught that we should be loving, kind, respectful, and compassionate; and he exemplified this behavior. Spiritual development was fostered pragmatically through practice as well as self-reflection and conversation. He gave freely without expectation of return; thus creating an ascending vortex for change with himself at the center. His energy still vibrates and resonates in those who saw his value and the blessings to be obtained through contact and connection with him.

Karmu used psychology as an agent in social change. He was deeply political and pressed his clients to better understand the political system, the political forces in play, and social history, especially as it applied to human oppression. He was deeply sensitive regarding man's inhumanity towards others and deeply committed to resolving these issues, regardless of how he was perceived.

There were no sacred cows when it came to Karmu's political opinions. He expressed his ideas directly and pressed you to develop your social self and your social interest. He expected everyone to become an agent for social change through daily interactions. He understood, like Adler, that our long experience of dependency fostered an inferiority complex in each individual that was overcome through active social agency. Few healing sessions were complete without a lesson in current politics – he would call people out and name names.

Karmu was a black man who played an active role in the liberation of Africans in America. He taught all clients the significance of race in American society and to address racial oppression through social action. No holds were barred, no villain unscathed, and certainly no blaming of the victim. He activated each individual's moral compass and gave it direction.

The deepest roots of the Karmu System are in ancient Egypt where the notion of a subtle system of energy channels arose. Karmu viewed the body as possessing channels through which energy flowed. He focused on energy centers and energy points at various locations along the body. The Egyptian system of medicine informed medical practices in the east and is the mother of acupuncture. Karmu appears to have learned energy healing approaches through an oral tradition.

He was identified as a healer in his childhood and his development as a healer was part of a long standing oral tradition. He also studied with many "root" doctors, including Gullah Geechee, Dr. Buzzard healers. Karmu believed that the source of healing was already inside the person and believed that his charisma and energy could assist in activating the healing of others. He assisted his clients in every arena of their lives.

Karmu operated within a traditional healing framework. He explored and developed a cosmic consciousness. He took the pain of others into his own body, transformed it, and articulated a divine mission to change the world. Various indigenous cultures around the world share the tradition wherein a person serves the community as a healer after a breakthrough from a mental, physical, or spiritual crisis. Karmu has been referenced as a wounded healer.

A shaman is identified as an individual who overcomes tremendous physical, mental, and spiritual obstacles – Karmu was probably no different. The person experiences an inner transformation and spiritual awakening of healing ability by transcending the pain of their wounds. A person could have a disability or a chronic illness and still achieve psychological wellness. A person can achieve tremendous psychological reserves by working through the liabilities of a "debilitating condition." This transformation appears to have occurred in Karmu and may help to account for the development of his cosmic consciousness.

Karmu applied psychological and philosophical principles in his approach to wellness. He was also known to go into trance for short periods of time to solve problems presented to him. Trance for Karmu was a meditative state devoid of thought, yet he came out with answers. He earned great respect among his peers by generously healing many people who had all kinds of physical, mental, spiritual ailments.

Karmu as a Model of Wellness

Karmu presented a system of healing for the attainment of wellness. Individuals like Karmu who manifest as spiritual teachers have been rare enough to warrant scientific study. They serve selflessly and show signs regarding who and what we all can become when our body, mind, and soul are in harmony.

Physically, Karmu became a professional boxer who fought the likes of the great Tiger Flowers. Theodore (Tiger) Flowers was the first black middleweight boxing champion. He claimed that title in 1926 after defeating Harry Greb. Mentally, he grew to become an integrated psychic who was such a dynamic figure that internationally renowned Sufi master teacher Murshid Samuel L. Lewis (Sufi Ahmed Murad Chisti) referred to him as the "Black Christ." Sufi Sam was a Zen Master and senior Sufi teacher who founded The Holy Order of Mans, the Dances of Universal Peace, and Sufi Ruhaniat International. Karmu embodied and taught the simple message that getting on a spiritual or religious path was more important than which path was chosen – he said that all spiritual and religious paths can lead to God.

Cosmic Consciousness

Cosmic consciousness was at the core of Karmu's "gift" and he often stated that he had access to the cosmic arena. Bucke viewed cosmic consciousness as an evolution of the soul that included intellectual illumination, moral exaltation, feelings of elevation, a sense of immortality, direction reception of God's will, elation, and joyousness. He described cosmic consciousness as perception and direct reception of divinity, composed of a sense of one's immortality and a sense of inter-connectedness with all beings.

He believed cosmic consciousness was an evolutionary process that will one day be commonplace. He conceptualized humanity as moving from simple consciousness to self-consciousness and, in rare instances, individuals achieve cosmic consciousness. He viewed intuition as the "mental component" of cosmic consciousness.

Bucke postulated cosmic consciousness as a holistic consciousness of the cosmos that people rarely achieved, but ultimately will impact all of humanity.

RELEVANT PSYCHOLOGICAL TRADITIONS

Analytical Psychology

Carl Gustav Jung was a Swiss born psychiatrist who integrated medicine, philosophy, and religion into his system of psychology. Jung became a student of Freudian psychoanalysis and with Freud's support, he was eventually elected chairman of the International Psychoanalytical Association. Freud ultimately opposed Jung's desire to integrate metaphysical ideas into psychoanalysis. Jung developed a more mystical version of psychoanalysis called analytical psychology (depth psychology) after he and Freud ended their six-year friendship and collaboration.

Jung rejected the striving for perfection and replaced it with the striving for wholeness in his theory of personality. He used art forms such as autobiographical writing, drawing, painting, poetry, and storytelling to help the individual gain greater understanding into self and move towards wholeness. Jung thought that achieving wholeness involved the development of our potentials, integrating our shadow into our persona, and addressing our complexes. It also involves developing our masculine side if we are females, our feminine side if we are males, and integrating these masculine/feminine qualities into the personality.

The purpose of life was to give it meaning. Meaning is generally found through the process of doing psychological and spiritual work. We cannot grow psychologically unless we grow spiritually, and we cannot attain our spiritual maturity unless we mature psychologically. Jung suggested that we accomplish our great work by becoming who and what we are meant to be. Self-realization is a central concept in analytical psychology.

Self-realization involves self-knowledge, illumination, and is both psychological and spiritual. Perfection involves identification with an ideal and attempts to realize that ideal, while wholeness incorporates ideals as goals, but striving is towards the realization of inherent potential.

Jung also incorporated the concept of synchronicity as the perception of meaningful coincidences in his psychological system. He believed that we live in a unified reality where everything is meaningful and nothing is meaningless. Each moment and event has its own deep reality. We live in a universe where coincidence is non-trivial. Divination produces knowledge, truth, and reality since there is no random occurrence from this perspective.

Western psychology embraced Freudian psychoanalysis and marginalized Jungian analytical psychology. The mystical nature of analytical psychology did not fit well with the materialist objective of suppressing metaphysics. However, analytical psychology provides insight into a meta-theory of psychological wellness since meaning, purpose, and self-realization are focal areas of psychological wellness.

Maslow's Self-Actualization

Humanistic psychology is phenomenological in that it emphasizes the subjective experience of the perceiver rather than a mechanistic approach based on objective analysis. Humanistic theorists adopted the striving towards wholeness as a central motivation in the development of personality.

Psychologists such as Abraham Maslow, Carl Rogers, and others referred to this motivation as the thriving for "self-actualization." Maslow's self-actualization construct appears to reflect an attempt to make Jung's self-realization concept more measurable. An actualizing person is a fully functioning individual who has identified her or his uniqueness and is expressing that uniqueness. Once activated, self-actualization is an on-going process of becoming. Self-actualization is both goal and process.

Maslow believed that the central goal in life was to actualize inherent potentials. He thought that individuals moved towards actualization sequentially by meeting and addressing a hierarchy of needs. He identified basic needs and growth needs as the two sets of needs. Maslow thought that once basic needs were met growth needs became salient. An individual must first address basic needs in order to move on towards growth needs.

Once physiological needs are adequately met, safety needs become salient. Once safety needs are met, individuals move on to the need for love and belonging. Once love and belonging are satisfied concern shifts to esteem needs. The highest stage is self-actualization or the striving to become who we were meant to be.

Maslow coined the term "peak experience" to refer to mystical experiences during which a person experiences intense happiness and well-being, a feeling of "unity with all things," and possibly the awareness of "ultimate truth." He suggested that self-actualizing individuals experienced more frequent episodes of peak experiences than those not self-actualizing. He also began work to integrate the concept of self-transcendence into his theory but died prior to the completion of this project. He intended to develop the concept of transcendence as the last stage of the hierarchy of needs.

Transpersonal Psychology

Maslow recognized a need for western psychology to more

fully integrate spiritual concepts into psychology and began development of a "fourth force" in psychology. Transpersonal psychology was to be a psychology centered in the cosmos that goes beyond personal experience. Transpersonal psychologists investigated phenomena such as transcendent states of mind, peak experience, and trance.

Maslow's effort towards constructing a "fourth force" in scientific psychology reflects his recognition that something was lacking in psychology. He perceived a void in the mechanistic reductionist tendencies of scientific psychology. His Transpersonal School of Psychology, however, was still individualistic, elitist, and fragmented. Transpersonal psychologists looked to the east for ideas and inspiration, but rarely have they looked to the African continent. Maslow did not explore the African subconscious mind in us all. Maslow's attempt at a fourth force in psychology may not have looked far enough.

The Concept of Flow

Maslow's investigations opened doors of scientific psychology to the concept of flow. Flow is the optimal experience that produces happiness and indicates that the person is self-actualizing. It is unclear whether flow is an aspect of the self, or the domain, since it appears to be more of an interaction of the two. To self-actualize one must develop the ego, transcend the ego by serving others, and flow.

Flow is the capacity to be in the ever-present moment. It requires skill obtained through disciplined work and the matching of skills with ideals and challenging goals. Flow has been found to occur in any type of activity that involves the right combination of challenge, skill, and feedback.

Csikszentmihalyi suggests that the flow applies on both the individual and the group (cultural) level.

The Concept of Trance

Maslow's investigations also opened the doors of scientific psychology to the concept of trance. Trance is an altered state of consciousness. Trance, also known as the hypnogogic state of consciousness, can be entered through various means such as meditation, dance, religious ecstasy, drumming, hypnosis, and so on. These activities can bring individuals into deeper, higher, and alternate states of consciousness.

Csikszentmihalyi observed that artists, poets, musicians, and other creative individuals could achieve trance and flow as they created. They themselves did not necessarily perceive the trance state or understand the process of getting there – they simply applied their craft. The distinction between trance and flow is unclear.

Complementary Medicine

Deepak Chopra is a contemporary medical doctor whose approach to medicine, health care, and psychology incorporates eastern philosophy and religion along with his western scientific training. His medical background, long list of books, and extensive lecturing has attracted interest and enthusiasm among readers, listeners, and patients.

He believes that success in life includes good health, energy, enthusiasm for life, fulfilling relationships, creative freedom, emotional and psychological stability, a sense of well-being, and peace of mind. All of these things are said to be possible if we nurture and cultivate our divinity. Seven of the principles he identified provide a roadmap for navigating life's journey toward these goals. According to Chopra:

1. Our spirit is a field of awareness that connects everything to everything instantly.

2. Our inner dialogue reflects our inner power:

   i. "I am independent of the good or the bad in people."

   ii. "I am neither superior nor inferior to other people."

   iii. "I have no desire to have power over, manipulation of or to control other people."

3. Our intentions have infinite organizing power.

4. I know how to rise above emotional turbulence through sobriety and witnessing.

5. Nurturing love and relationships is the most important activity of my soul.

6. I embrace the masculine and feminine in my own being.

7. I am aware of the conspiracy of improbabilities and there is no such thing as coincidence.

He contends that success is achieved by asking and answering two key questions: How can I help? How can I be of service? He believes that when we connect our talents and purpose to serving humanity by asking and answering these key questions, abundance and wellness unfold.

We express our divinity when we express our unique talents in service to humanity. We self-actualize and transcend our ego when we do what we came to do in service to humanity. Chopra believes that: Everyone has a purpose in life... a unique gift or special talent to give to others. That when we blend this unique talent with service to others, we experience the ecstasy and exaltation of our spirit, which is the ultimate goal of all goals.

Chopra's work fits well into the Humanistic and Positive Psychology School. This work complements psychology and medicine in America. It provides valuable insights from an eastern perspective and serves as an adjunct to western approaches.

Myers' Optimal Psychology

Linda Myers proposed a theory of optimal psychology with worldview as the central concept. Two major worldviews are explicated in her work: one is said to be optimal while the other is considered to be sub-optimal. The optimal worldview is based in a unity of material and spiritual reality wherein spirit is primary and the individual experiences a loss of the individualized ego. The individual experiences the harmony of collective identity and oneness with the source of all good. This interconnectedness is the essence of the African-centered cultural paradigm.

The sub-optimal worldview emphasizes a mind/matter duality that fragments and segments reality and people with an emphasis on material reality. The suboptimal worldview fosters racism, sexism, classism, and general unhappiness. An optimal worldview fosters wellness in the individual and contributes to optimal outcomes in the world, according to Myers. Optimal theory also provides therapeutic strategies for bringing an individual back into harmony with self and others. This spiritually-based value system is said to foster psychological wellness in the individual.

The belief systems analysis scale (BSAS) was developed in the context of optimal theory to operationalize and measure the African-centered and Eurocentric worldviews. Findings from research in optimal psychology suggest that psychological wellness involves a stable sense of self, healthy ego development, and the development of cultural identity. The African-centered worldview is thought to emphasize values that cultivate societies that foster healthy ego identity and psychological wellness.

Racial Identity Theory

Cross's racial identity theory was developed to better understand black people: however, all people have ethnicity and ethnic identity models have been developed for many ethnic groupings. Developmental theory highlights the role of ethnicity in psychosocial development. Strong racial identity is a factor which protects African Americans from the negative consequences of self-perceived discrimination.

Erik Erikson explored the role society plays in the development of individual identity. He developed a stage model that provides a roadmap for developing individuals with strong healthy egos and the prevention of psychological disorder. Erikson's model spawned a great deal of ethnic identity research (although he himself did not directly address the role of ethnicity in identity formation).

Other psychological researchers such as Cross extended Erikson's model to ethnic and cultural identity. Ethnic identity is a constituent of ego identity and plays a role in psychological wellness. A clear sense of identity has been a focal area of psychological wellness research.

Resiliency

Resiliency has been defined as the ability to bounce back from difficult situations and the ability to respond to changing circumstances effectively. It has been thought of as a self-righting capacity that enables an individual to develop healthy attitudes, self-esteem, and competency. Personal and individual factors that foster success are labeled as protective. Protective factors are thought to foster resiliency.

Henderson described protective factors as characteristics within the individual or environment that minimized the negative impact of stressful events and situations. Research on resiliency represents a shift from deficit thinking to an emphasis on individual strengths and well-being.

There are critical junctures in a person's life where important decisions need to be made. Resilient individuals emerge from these critical times transformed into even more resilient people. While there has been research linking racial identity and resiliency, more research is needed to strengthen the link between racial identity and resilience. Resilient individuals are better adapted to the times in a world of rapid change.

Adlerian Individual Psychology

Alfred Adler's social interest concept seems particularly relevant to our understanding of psychological wellness. Adler regarded social interest as a human potential and theorized that the development of social interest was motivated by efforts to overcome feelings of inferiority. He thought that individuals inevitably experience feelings of inferiority due to the long period of dependency on others during infancy and childhood.

He conceptualized the development of social interest as the successful resolution to inferiority feelings. He saw the development of social interest as the solution to the problem. Adler hypothesized that failure to fully resolve these feelings could result in a mistaken style of life. Examples of mistaken styles of life would include criminal behavior, neurosis, psychosis, alcoholism, and so on.

Fostering social interest may provide a protective factor which helps to ameliorate risk factors and optimizes psychological wellness. Resilience occurs when there are cumulative protective factors. These factors are likely to play a greater role the higher an individual's exposure to cumulative risk factors. Higher levels of resilience were found to be associated with higher levels of social interest in a sample of black college students.

Self-efficacy

Albert Bandura's social learning theory has become a dominant theory in modern psychology. Bandura postulated that the future influences the present in such a way that our goals for the future influence how we behave in the present. A central concept in social learning theory is self-efficacy. Self-efficacy is the self-perception that we have the capacity to do what is necessary in order to achieve the outcomes we desire.

Social learning theory and self-efficacy research has important implications for our understanding of psychological wellness. Self-efficacy beliefs have been shown to determine whether coping behavior will be initiated, how much effort will be expended, and how long it will be sustained.

Researchers have also found that high self-efficacy can help prevent relapse to unhealthy behavior.

The Take Away

The current survey suggests the importance of self-realization, cultural identity, resiliency, self-efficacy, social interest, flow, and trance in models of psychological wellness. These variables emerge from a survey of a large body of relevant literature and placing findings in the context of an individual life. Actualizing individuals who are high in cultural identity, self-efficacy, resiliency, and social interest can experience high levels of cosmic consciousness and more frequent flow in life.

Karmu exhibited many of the characteristics Bucke associated with cosmic consciousness. Group studies and an individual case were selected that built on subjective a priori ideas about psychological wellness. As such, empirical research is needed to validate this conceptual model.

Working Hypotheses

Several models of psychological wellness define wellness as the movement towards higher levels of optimal functioning. The model of psychological wellness presented in this chapter suggests that individuals who are psychologically well grow in the development of cosmic consciousness. Like resiliency, psychological wellness predicts the ability to bounce back from the calamities of life.

The current chapter is speculative and theoretical. The intent is to explore new ground in psychological wellness theory and research. Optimal theory and the African subconscious mind were considered in the development of the current wellness model. The working hypothesis of the present formulation is that psychological wellness involves growth towards cosmic consciousness.

Correspondingly, movement along the continuum from self-consciousness towards cosmic consciousness facilitates psychological wellness. Going into trance and meditative states may offer benefits towards the development of a cosmic consciousness. A comprehensive understanding of the dimensional structure of psychological wellness is under construction and valid measures of this construct are needed.

Meta-Theory Considerations

A meta-theory of psychological wellness would integrate wellness constructs and specify the relationships between aspects of the self and aspects of domains of life. The conceptual model presented here is simply a creative suggestion. The approach presented here integrates ideographic and nomothetic data. Similar models could be constructed and structural models could be formulated.

A meta-theory formulation of psychological wellness with empirical data could potentially be a powerful tool for understanding psychological wellness. However, science does not appear to be close to measuring cosmic consciousness and valid measures of psychological wellness are still needed. Work in positive psychology sheds light on the concept of psychological wellness from a scientific perspective.

Unfortunately, positive psychology has failed to integrate knowledge from the African-centered paradigm. African-centered psychology and optimal theory are developments that can provide psychological insights that may foster a meta-theory of psychological wellness and a truly integrative positive psychology movement.

Karmu served as a living, breathing example of a person who achieved psychological wellness and provides a model of human possibility since he mastered the integration of mind, body, and soul. He also presented an African-centered system of healing for the attainment of psychological and overall wellness – a system that is still applicable in today's complex post-modern society.

ơ ơ ơ

12

ANCIENT EGYPTIAN MAGIC AND SHAMANISM

THE TERM "shamanism" is reported to have come to us from Siberia and Central Asia through Russia from the Tungusic saman. The highest development of shamanic practice was probably in ancient Egypt even though Atlantian High Priests and Priestess also performed the functions that we would today term shamanic.

Karmu's work as a healer was rooted in the medicinal practices of the ancient Egyptian physicians. Ancient Egyptian healing systems migrated throughout traditional societies and a great many names developed for the practice. Medicine Man, Physician, Obeah Man, Witch-doctor, Curandero, Faith Healer, Voodoo Priest and many other terms have been employed. The builders of ancient Egyptian civilization were the people and the country that became known as Kemet (KMT). The term KMT translates into land of the Blacks.

Anthropologists have identified the practice of shamanism in locations as diverse as Africa, Asia, and the Indian cultures of North and South America. Shamanism has taken on many forms and is viewed in both negative and positive terms.

The system of healing practiced by Karmu was a modern

extension of the ancient Egyptian healing practices. The wounded healer is an archetype of the shamanic path that usually begins with an initiatory crisis which commonly involves a physical illness or psychological crisis. The details of Karmu's "wounding" were kept secret by him. The obvious "wound" in Karmu's life was the "invisibility" hosted upon him by a society that failed to acknowledge the special gifts he offered to the communities in which he lived and practiced. The shamanic journey involves a "breakdown" which functions as a "breakthrough." Karmu was probably no different in this regard.

Ancient Energy Healing

The ancient Egyptians had a form of medicine involving clinical diagnosis and treatment that today would be called alternative medicine. These ancient Africans were among the first to manipulate energy to promote healing. They believed that the life-force or Ka is the energy that animates the body and circulates throughout the body. They viewed humans as beings of light that radiate and transmit light energy. They viewed the body as possessing channels through which energy flowed. Blockage or stagnation of Ka was thought to cause illness and disease. Various implements were used to clear blockage and move energy through the body.

Energy and oxygen were recognized by ancient Africans as healing forces. The vibratory frequency generated by pyramids was said to create an oxygen-ionized environment by liberating oxygen from carbon dioxide molecules. Imhotep was a surgeon who conducted surgery in special chambers in the ionized atmosphere generated by the structure of the pyramids. Healing through the energy of sound was also a part of this process. It has been speculated that pyramids were energy production, storage, and distribution facilities and that special chambers in the pyramid were tuned to frequencies that helped restore the body to the correct harmonic frequency.

Magical practices were deemed essential and the power of the mind was actively harnessed as an integral part of ancient healing systems. Psychological processes within the patient played an important role in healing. Hypnosis, trance, chanting, meditation, spells, amulets, rituals, and many forms of magic were employed. Egyptians used sleep temples as places to activate the psycho-spiritual powers of the patient's mind. Citizens visited the temples, were placed in trance, given suggestions, and instructed to speak with gods to obtain healing and solutions to their problems. Dream interpretation was conducted, and sleep through the night in designated temples was the ritual designed for communication with gods. Psychological and physical ailments were treated holistically.

Egyptian Magic

Ancient Egyptians practiced an approach to healing, medicine, and psychiatry that was tied to the diagnosis and included the study of human anatomy. These practices predated Hippocrates and other western medical practitioners by over 35 centuries. Clinical methods were used that involved an examination, diagnosis, prognosis, and treatment.

Ancient Egyptians called medicine the necessary art and this art involved various forms of magic. The Egyptian priest Imhotep, rather than Hippocrates, is the true father of this "necessary art". Magic, science, and religion were wedded together, and the art of medicine was the best representation of this union. Ancient Egyptian concepts and practices laid a foundation for modern medicine and psychiatry.

Heka

Heka was one of the Egyptian words for magic and the most important god associated with magic. Akhu was another word for magical power. Magic was viewed as a cosmic force used to create and maintain the world. The word Heka also means activating the Ka.

Egyptians thought activating the Ka, or soul, was how magic worked. Magic was a power of the soul and medicine was a form of magic. Egyptian priests were trained in magic and could become practitioners through religion, medicine, and other forms of magic. Egyptians believed that with Heka they could influence the gods and gain protection, healing, and transformation since health and wholeness were sacred to Heka.

Most Egyptian physicians were priests. Physicians were frequently trained in the "per ankh" or "house of life". Djehuti is recognized as the god of magic, the god of medicine, and patron of all physicians. Many physicians were trained in the temples of Djehuti.

Sekhmet, the lion-headed destroyer of mankind, was the primary goddess associated with physicians. Physicians were often trained in her temples. Sekhmet could send disease upon men. Isis was also associated with medicine and physicians. She resurrected her own husband Osiris and healed a child through the laying on of hands. Other divine patrons of medicine were Osiris, Horus, Neith, Hathor, Bes, Thoueris, Khnum and Hekhet.

Magic played a key role in ancient Egyptian life and treatments were infused with magic. Religion and magic were wedded together in the conceptualization and practice of medicine. Medicine combined physical and spiritual components, since humans were seen as a combination of spiritual and material forces. Disease was seen as a material reflection of cosmic struggle between health-giving forces and toxic ones. Illness was viewed as having a spiritual dimension and was often treated with spells.

Sekhmet

Incantations were often performed to activate the substances used to treat illness. A poultice of ostrich egg shell treated with a spell was applied to the forehead of a man with a skull injury, since the shell is round and looks like a skull (a case referenced in the Edwin Smith papyrus). This suggests a type of sympathetic magic since the egg shell resembles the skull. The attack upon an enemy "by proxy" through the manipulations performed on a wax figure made in the shape of the enemy is another example of sympathetic magic indicated in the Edwin Smith papyrus.

Magic was an integral part of Egyptian medicine and a combination of clinical and magical procedures complimented each other. The Egyptian medical pharmacopeia was quite large, consisting of as many as 1000 animal, plant, and mineral products to treat illness. Plant essences were used to treat diseases. Poppy extract might be used to treat colicky babies. Ox livers were a rich source of vitamin A used to treat night blindness. Scurvy was treated with onions, a source of vitamin C. Garlic and onions were commonly used and considered sacred. Magical perfumes were reported to enhance intuition, foresight, and visions. Remedies were dispensed in pills, enemas, suppositories, infusions, and elixirs. Acupuncture, homeopathy, and yoga were also practiced.

Spells were cast by the officiating priest, either in his name, or in the name of a god. The word was synonymous with the deed and with Heka saying it made it so. The Edwin Smith papyrus refers to a spell used along with a cream to make an old man young. There was performance or ritual in magic and there were water cures that involved ritual. Priests might pour water over a statue, collect the water and give it to a person who was ill to drink.

Magic was based on the premise that there is an invisible realm that affects the physical realm such that manipulating the invisible forces could lead to effects in the material world. Another basic principle was that like could cure like. Magical ability was assumed to come from individual mastery of life. Moral development was an important part of the individual development required for the mastery of magic.

The practice of magic in ancient Egypt was based on the following assumptions, according to Ghalioungui:

- There is an immaterial force permeating the universe.

- There is a correspondence between the macrocosm and the microcosm such that changes in one realm affected changes in the other.

- Like evokes like. For example, in Egyptian medicine if the vagina was emitting a foul smell, the cure was to fumigate it with meat that had that smell.

- Events that have followed each other in the past will follow each other in the future.

- A body remains forever linked to any fragment detached from it, or that touched it. Hence, it was possible to act on a person through items of clothing, hair, nail clipping, and so on.

- The dead carry on their lives in another state of being and can return in the form of dreams or ghosts.

Spells, incantations, rituals, amulets, charms, wax figures, and water infused by pouring it over a statue were all used to bring about medical cures. Amulets were small objects typically used for protection. Knots, that played the role of a god, could become the vehicle of the magician's power. A harmful being, in the form of an illness, could be commanded, threatened, or opposed, and immunity could be asserted.

Certain medications were considered to work by absorbing evil, or by transferring it to another being. A headache might be treated by rubbing the aching side of the head with the head of a fried fish to transfer the pain from the person to the head of the fish (transference). A whole class of procedures was based on identification with a god.

For example, the magician might state, "Look, I am Horus, beware lest the gods suffer, for then will darkness fall, clouds will obscure the sky, and water shall overspread the earth."

Magic became discredited and suppressed over the ages in western societies, but it still exists in many modern systems including psychology, religion, and medicine. Placebos are a modern form of magic and can be used to treat conditions when combined with "proper" instructions (e.g., the use of sugar pills). Empirical evidence demonstrates that significant numbers of people respond to inert substances they ingest when they believe they received an active ingredient. Experimenter effects, expectancy bias, demand characteristics, hypnosis, and placebo effects are scientifically verified psychological phenomena that exhibit a mysterious and often unexplainable magical quality.

Quantum mechanics is revealing that energy is generated by intention, suggestion, and expectation. Belief operates as an organizing principle and a self-fulfilling prophecy attracting that which facilitates manifestation of the belief. Continued attention to the belief maintains the energy and facilitates the intention of the belief. People often take the position that "if I see it, I will believe it". But, it isn't that "seeing is believing". It's the other way around – believing is seeing. Once you believe it you can conceive it and actualize it.

An African-centered View

Medicine was a form of magic in many ancient societies, and placebos were an integral part of any treatment plan. Ancient African's believed in Nommo or the power of the word and medicine was considered to be impotent without the power of the word. Treating the mind benefits the body since mind and body are inextricably connected. Medical practitioners should inspire faith, hope, and belief in the recovery since these psychological components are vital forces in the treatment of any health condition. Metaphysical African philosophy reminds us that all is Spirit. Practitioners who inspire hope are incorporating an important ingredient since hope has life enhancing benefits.

Ancient Egyptian priests were trained in many arts and sciences including magic and medicine. Magic was an integral part of the Egyptian worldview and Egyptian doctors, physicians, and priests practiced magic. The Egyptians paved the way for the modern study and practice of medicine and psychiatry; however, the magic of these ancient Africans has been suppressed and its place in modern medicine has not been duly acknowledged.

Magic in the modern era has become a form of illusion while true magic goes unacknowledged. Spirituality, magic, and religion did not differ in ancient Egyptian societies. Medical and psychiatric systems in the west still include many forms of ancient Egyptian magic.

Shamanism is a spirit-based form of healing practiced by many indigenous cultures that may have deep roots in ancient Egyptian magic. Modern cultures tend to use the term medicine, but irrespective of preferred terminology, good health and healing are blessings that come from understanding and harmonizing the body's innate intelligence with the laws of nature and the principles of the universe.

Violations of nature's laws can foster ill health. Many theories and systems exist to explain how illness and healing occurs. Each approach to health and wellness seems capable of curing some conditions, but not others. Physicians and other health practitioners play a critical role in the healing process, but the source of healing appears to be within the person with the malady.

Western medicine encourages people to believe they have a condition that must be managed, treated, or cured, rather than a lack of harmony that is compelling them to make changes in their lives. People are taught to have something removed surgically or to take a pill rather than change the factors causing the condition. A change in thinking and feeling is often a critical step in alleviating a medical condition (as empirical evidence of the placebo effect suggests).

It appears that the major curative agent may be within rather than outside the person and that healing is a spiritual journey back to Spirit. A paradigm shift in thinking that integrates the western and eastern approaches with a greater emphasis on the prevention of illness and disease is indicated.

Karmu practiced an alternative form of healing that can be called energy healing. His approach was holistic with roots in Asia and Africa. As a shaman he traveled between the human and spiritual worlds to treat problems of mind, body, and soul. Karmu also played an active role in the liberation of black people. He taught his patients the significance of race in American society, strategies for dealing with the stresses of racial oppression, and served as a model for helping oppressed people deal with the pressures of racism, sexism, and classism.

He was sensitive to the problems associated with structural violence and helped people navigate the daily trials and tribulations presented in American society. He functioned as a shaman who cared deeply about people and generously helped legions of people. He transitioned from this world relatively unacknowledged, given the magnitude of his contribution and his work.

CB CB CB

13

KARMU AND
SHAMANIC HEALING

THIS CHAPTER brings the experience with Karmu and Shamanic Healing full circle. These reflections place us in the same space. The world has changed, yet remains the same. We all still desire to be loved. We want to be respected and have our worth affirmed. We want to be valued. We all still dream of a better world. We still cling to the dream of world peace. We still seek purpose. We want to be well – mentally, physically and spiritually.

Karmu was attuned to this. We are all connected in one way or another in our desires and motivations as it relates to personal health, yet we walk our individualized pathways. I was honored with a path that led me to Karmu.

The book has a section that questioned our conscious constructs of wellness and disease. We also conclude with the same challenge. What does it truly mean to experience wellness? Healing is a process that has high and low tides in its evolution. As such, we must remain open to contemporary advances in healing practices, yet not err in discounting historical knowledge and leanings that have served us well in building a firm foundation in our personal and collective journey towards holistic health and wellness. Healing has a history. Karmu vigorously embraced this.

There is persistent vacillation between Western medicine, historical, traditional and natural healing practices. Academicians attempt to form a bridge between the physical and the psychic interplay of active healing, as they juxtapose theory with practical applications. Too often we are confronted with a "one or the other" proposition. Further, the comparison is frequently housed in very limiting linear suppositions.

However, there is space – to varying degrees – for the embrace of different approaches. More attention needs to be afforded to the needs of the whole person; after all, the human body as a canvas, is large and complex. One's body, like the mind and spirit has unlimited potential. Therefore, wellness and efforts to attain it should not be regulated to simplistic boxes of understanding and actualization – Karmu conveyed this.

Any honest movement towards holistic health cannot be undertaken without attending to the mind, body, and spirit – since they are all connected, they must be dealt with collectively. The mind is expansive and provides us with the opportunity to reach different levels.

Karmu was a thinker who functioned on a higher cosmic plane. He held audiences with those well beyond the confines of the academy. They consisted of gurus, spiritual teachers, shaman and other individuals existing on different cosmic evolutionary levels. He had immense psychic sensitivity and energy that you could feel. This energy was strong, almost palpable. You changed in his presence, becoming lifted to a higher place after interacting with him. You never left his presence the same as you had arrived.

Karmu would travel in the spirit realm, visiting other people while sleeping or in a trance-like state. He insisted that the spirit had a lot of truth to share and helps in expanding our knowledge and understanding. He was the consummate storyteller and giver who never ceased from giving. He often shared how his visit to other worlds and realms of existence was where he would at times acquire information needed to help certain individuals who sought his assistance. He would go to asleep in front of you, then in a few minutes awake and tell you what to do and how to do it. He always provided practical assistance.

To Karmu everything was energy. He had an enormous spirit. He enjoyed life. Small gatherings became a party. He would address theoretical constructs, quote philosophers and recite poetry. Karmu was gregarious and spoke fast. The private interactions with him, this spirit-filled man, became a precious jewel. It was a gift which continues to provide insight so many years later. This indeed, is what the spirit, not the physical affords us.

His strong desire to help others was equally matched with his strong physical presence. He had fought professionally as a boxer and had strong hands. He dominated space, was highly energetic, magnetic and held the center of attention – even if he was not, he seemed at least six feet tall. There was space for all in his circle. Everyone felt a special and unique relationship with him.

Karmu felt that the spirit was a vessel for the body. We conveyed that we all had to continuous work on our vessel. He insisted that one's skin should be taken care of, as well as the need to get proper exercise. The wellness of our bodies, to him, was just as important as the mind and the spirit. In efforts to heal the body, he would commune with other entities in the cosmic arena. He would share the results of these visits. He had received training from his father, who was trained by other healers and islanders. His mother was also a healer. Karmu did not station himself on this side of reality. He traveled beyond physical planes and experienced other realms of existence. The body, he shared, was a temple.

I have strong memories of the gatherings in his home, the red medicine that he would pass around in Dixie cups and his generosity of spirit. He encouraged me to seek a doctoral degree. Our relationship evolved into one in which I became his admiring student. I sought his guidance and consultation. He always delivered.

I often ponder whether Karmu was a man ahead of his time. Were the world, modern medicine, and our modern mindset ready for him? Then, at times I rest firmly on the possibility that he was indeed here at his appointed time, where and exactly when he was supposed to be. He has been, and remains so, a vital part of the "foundational work" of holistic wellness and healing. I, in addition to the various larger community of healers, am better because he came this way. We became more whole through his presence among us. There is an indebtedness that can only be reconciled by acknowledging those who came before and with us on this wellness journey and by placing more steps on this path through research and the advocacy for natural healing remedies and practices. Karmu always acknowledged those that came before him.

What I miss most about him is the physical Karmu; being able to turn directly to him when seeking solutions for wellness and balance. Karmu transitioned in 1989. At times when I am threatened or disturbed with some type of disease or health challenge, I look for him; not in flesh, rather in cosmic energy, harbored among my most precious memories. More importantly, I find him everywhere: the wrestling of leaves when gently lifted and tossed by wind; the glow of sunsets in summer; the stillness of daybreak in winter; and in the promised return of spring when the Earth is renewed with buds of flowers and the songs of birds fill the air; finding him because I still speak his name – the healer, my friend. Karmu!

CB CB CB

14
THE KARMU HEALING SYSTEM OVERVIEW

ONE FOUNDATION of the Karmu System was a diet designed around each individual's biochemistry, constitution, and health conditions. Karmu saw diet as a critical, but individual matter and tended to consult with his patients about the specific diet that would be best for them. He always had a pot of soup in his refrigerator to share that was made up of basic foods such as onions, garlic, cayenne pepper, sweet potatoes, and so on. In my case he recommended a lot of foods that supported brain and immune function. Karmu also used herbs and supplements and often encouraged people to stop taking certain medications.

Detoxification was another foundation. Virtually everyone was expected to detox. His most common form of detox was by soaking in blue medicine baths and blue medicine foot soaks. In my case, he suggested colonics to cleanse the bowels. Karmu had general procedures that were ultimately tailored to individual needs.

Karmu referred to another of his basic approaches as the "laying on of hands." He used this terminology to refer to his method of massage. Massage involved manipulating nerve centers, pressure points, and trigger points. He believed in the notion of energy pathways and energy centers in the body. He would focus on some areas and points, depending on individual's needs, but he believed in facilitating energy flow throughout the entire body. He would tap the body, pound the body, pretty much whatever he felt was needed to unblock the energy and keep it flowing.

Karmu believed in "penetrating the subconscious mind" and willing the person to get better, do better and be better. He did this verbally through encouragement, flattery, inspirational words, compliments, and pretty much anything that would make a person feel good. But when he deemed it necessary he might verbally "knock you down a few pegs." Most people who came around him left feeling uplifted. Charisma was one of Karmu's most visible gifts. He believed in the power of laughter and wanted to make people laugh and smile. He encouraged everyone to express their emotions and he provoked laughter – the louder you laughed the happier he became.

Karmu believed in physical exercise and encouraged everyone to be active. He taught a variety of exercises that a person could even do in bed. Fun, adequate sleep, and relaxation were also encouraged by Karmu. His system was not complicated and was fairly basic, however, Karmu himself was a vital ingredient.

Lastly, although Karmu did not advocate any particular religion, he taught that all religions were paths to God. He said it didn't matter which spiritual path a person chose, what mattered was that each person chose a path to follow. Faith in a higher power was essential to this system of Shamanic Healing.

CS CS CS

15

THE LIVES
KARMU TOUCHED...

HERE WE have different voices from individuals who expressed their personal experiences and sentiments regarding Karmu and his healing work with them. There is an inherent danger in listening to only one voice in any situation. The experiences that have been conveyed thus far have been authentic and personal. Yet, it is important to include other voices and threads of truth. While testimonials are anecdotal rather than scientific, Karmu's concern was not with science, it was with helping people.

On one occasion he had his assistant produced three large cardboard boxes of writings for me to read. The boxes included all kinds of writings from people who had visited him over the years. There were scholarly articles, journal entries, and creative works, but mostly they were testimonials. I read enough of them to get an idea of what was in the boxes. Most of the writings were testimonials that individuals wrote about the experiences they had with Karmu.

Karmu touched the lives of many people and the inclusion of all of their testimonies — including the ones that I heard personally – is far beyond the scope of this book. Visitors saw Karmu in many different ways. The following sample of testimonials provide a range of experiences that will bring you closer to understanding the man, his system for healing, and how he impacted the lives he touched.

CB CB CB

INTERVIEW WITH ONE OF KARMU'S CLIENTS

Ricardo: So, are the ailments you came to Karmu for cleared up?

Client: Sort of stable. Karmu has increased the healing process tremendously. Absolutely tremendously, and I'm now what you call basically healthy. I just get these spasms every now and then because I over-work. I work too much and Karmu calls me on it.

Karmu: We have an exchange and we also exchange energy. I can hold her in my arms and in 20 minutes she's like new.

Client: Oh, yeah! I can feel it, he is now working on a rash, a demon, that I've got, that was due to emotional strain, it was due to physiological things, it was due to extreme stress, due to over-work, and just some foolish things I knew better about and didn't listen to, and on one hand he removed a blockage here in my chest, it was really intense, I was having chest pains, and he opened it up, and my whole left arm got real painful. It was real intense and I passed out, but it opened it up and since then I've made tremendous progress. A week ago my face was, what color was my face Karmu?

Karmu: Red.

Client: Well it was more than red, it was scarlet and black and so puffy at times that I couldn't really see through my eyes and now it's like I have new skin.

Ricardo: How often do you come here?

Client: As often as I can, I come about once a week.

Karmu: She heals me you know. We have a thing between us that means we have to stay together for another 30 or 40 years at least.

Client: That's because he can't get rid of me.

Karmu: It's because whatever I need I can get from her. If I need encouragement I can get it. She's always there and I've come to depend on her. She's a part of my life.

Ricardo: You're referring to that exchange that goes on between you two.

Karmu: There's a spiritual and physical exchange. I boost her up to the world and she can feel it. She goes higher and she is going to rebuild the state of Wyoming for us.

Client: He's my natural high. Ha! ha! ha! ha!

03 03 03

INTERVIEW WITH SANDRA FRAZER (SISTER OF THE AUTHOR)

Ricardo: How were you introduced to Karmu?

Sandra: You introduced me to him in October of 1983. I wanted to do some healing work around gaining confidence.

Ricardo: Was he a healer, in your mind?

Sandra: Yes, that's why I wanted to do some work with him.

Ricardo: Why do you think he attracted so many patients?

Sandra: There are a lot of people looking for alternative help.

Ricardo: What do you see as the source of his ability to help people?

Sandra: I believe he had healing powers, and his own perception of how to help others.

Ricardo: Is this an ability anyone can have or was he special?

Sandra: I would say he was unique. I don't know if everyone has this ability. From my experience with him, I saw him study people. He helped people understand their own potential. Karmu was acutely aware of himself and his ability.

Ricardo: Did he have a gift or was it his ability developed?

Sandra: I think it was developed.

Ricardo: What's your most vivid memory of Karmu?

Sandra: I remember the work he did on me. He once had me try to do some healing work on him. I remember believing in him and in his capability. I don't think he was ordinary. He was extraordinary. I think he really wanted to help people and see them well. He was concerned about his fellow men.

Ricardo: Do you remember any of his sayings?

Sandra: He called people a triple movie star. He was real bright that way, always lifting people's spirit. He always tried to encourage people.

Ricardo: Do you feel he influenced you in any way?

Sandra: I guess my beliefs. I remember there were people who lived in his house or stopped through who could be negative about what he was doing. I felt their negativity brought people down and didn't help. I think if more people were like Karmu the world would be a better place. I was looking at the number of people like Karmu in the world and I haven't seen a lot like him. It's sad because it's all about money now.

෬ ෬ ෬

INTERVIEW WITH A CAMBRIDGE WOMAN WHO KNEW KARMU

Ricardo: How were you introduced to Karmu?

Client: I met Karmu because my housemate Janice was going to him for healings and blue medicine. Many of my housemates eventually went to him and it became a place where I would see Karmu, hang out with him, and other people from the neighborhood.

Ricardo: Why do you think he attracted so many patients?

Client: I think Karmu's warmth, humor, accessibility, generosity drew people to him. People tended to feel better just being with him because he was such a force of nature, funny, loving, and confident in his healing abilities.

Ricardo: Did Karmu have special healing abilities or what his ability commonplace?

Client: I heard lots of stories about Karmu healing people of cancer, when western medicine had failed them. I could never bring myself to drink blue medicine, but I bathed in it quite a lot and I felt better after seeing Karmu. I never saw him for anything life threatening, but things like the flue, a bad cough, stuff like that.

Ricardo: Was he the real thing?

Client: I think he was the real thing, and fell into the category of a faith healer. He healed with his energy, which was lively and caring, earthy and full of humor. Getting people to laugh and open up especially when they weren't feeling well was a big part of his appeal. He knew how to ease people's suffering, to set them at ease, to help them open up and talk about what was bothering them, he had a roaring laugh and a big barrel chest and belly, strong arms, kind of like a Sumo wrestler, but not at all intimidating.

Ricardo: Was he a great human being or an ordinary person?

Client: He was an ordinary man, living very simply, with an unusual amount of vim.

Ricardo: What is your most vivid memory of Karmu?

Client: I was feeling suddenly really crumby so I went to see Karmu. I had seen him at least six times in the past and he had never said to me what he said this particular time. He checked me out, asked me a bunch of questions, and suddenly he pinned me with his eyes and asked my pointedly, when no one else was in the room, if I had recently performed oral sex on a man. I said yes. He asked me if it was the first time I'd been with him. I said yes. He asked me if I'd swallowed any of his semen and I said yes. He told me this man was troubled and I had taken on his negative energy when I swallowed his semen and that I was not to do this again unless I was very sure a man's energy was pure. This was in the 70s before AIDs and the man I'd been intimate with had been celibate and a yogi for quite a while when I met him. I forget what remedy Karmu gave me or told me to take, but it left a lasting impression on me.

Ricardo: Do you recall any of Karmu's sayings?

Client: I remember every time I saw Karmu near the end of a session he would laugh, thump himself on the chest and thunder: How can we lose with the system we use!

Ricardo: Karmu seemed to be many things to many people. How do you regard him? Teacher? Healer? Guru? Etc. Please explain.

Client: Definitely not my guru. I've had a guru and Karmu was not this to me. Not a teacher either, although I suspect he was to you because you lived in his home and were a lot closer to him than I was. I'd say he was a faith healer.

ᘓ ᘓ ᘓ

CAMBRIDGE WOMAN'S PERSONAL TESTIMONY

I'm 57 years old, have lived in Cambridge since the late 70s, in the part of town now known as Riverside, where Karmu lived. I am a singer, songwriter, supporting myself as a chef. A garden and flower designer, and realtor over the years while continuing to compose and sing. I got into organic gardening, whole foods, and holistic healing in my early 20s. Although I believe in having a good primary care physician keeping tabs on my health, I tend to maintain my health through nutrition, exercise, meditation, singing, herbs, homeopathy and acupuncture.

Most people think I'm 10-15 years younger than I am and I attribute this to genes, lifestyle and a positive attitude. I have always reached out to healers when out of balance or ill. In general I'm healthy but I've been gravely ill and injured a few times. Finding the right people to help me heal and being willing to face my inner demons and emotional challenges with honesty, courage and compassion has made all the difference in my healing process and soul's journey.

I write songs about what I encounter along the way and although personal, they are universal. My 14-year-old son has been raised on organic whole foods, close to nature and music since he was a baby. He gets homeopathic remedies, herbs and acupuncture treatments on the rare occasions when he is ill. Twice in his life he's taken antibiotics. I've consulted a medical intuitive who's a friend of the family, when my son or I have had something chronic or difficult to diagnose.

I feel blessed that Nina is there for us when we need her. I also feel blessed to have an amazing primary care doctor who is a healer, teacher and jazz pianist. I am part of a long time Vipassana meditation class in Cambridge, taught by an old friend who is an inspiring teacher. This path, deepened by the teachings of people like Pema Chodron, plays an important part in my worldview and approach to my own being. As one of my songs says:

It's all about connection,
The simple joy to be
Standing in your shoes
With authenticity.

Dear Karmu,

I am the young woman – the writer – who went to the hospital for a bone marrow transplant, last November. I came to you, and I come to you again, with thanks. Often, I think of you and as you might expect, I can't stop the smile that comes with the thought. I try to tell people about you but I find "telling is insufficient." I risk the danger of sounding trite, and everyone has the usual reaction: "Faith healer? You must have been desperate, etc…" I was desperate, but to me, that doesn't matter. We come to our deepest realizations in moments of desperation.

I have been a wonderful success at the hospital – a walking miracle. I have had no complication. And now, I am working at the hospital doing research on the disease I had. I talk with patients who have what I had and I encourage them to believe in their will, in positive thinking, and in healing-type imagery. I have to be a little discreet about it because there is a lot of resistance to these "weird, hippy-like methods."

I admire you, respect you, because you always encourage me to follow my heart, to do what I felt was best. I chose the hospital route because it was what I was brought up with; but knowing I had seen you, felt you, made a huge difference in life. I will be there to see you within the next month. I was reading some of your "propaganda" tonight and couldn't resist writing.

Affectionately,

Jessica

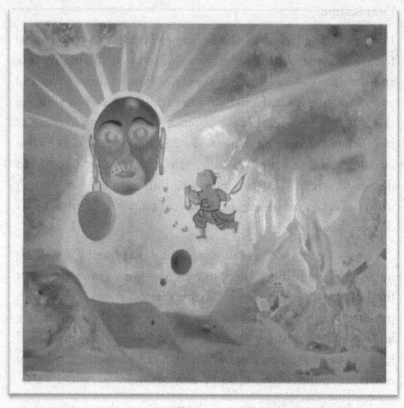

Karmu said Look to the East – oil on canvas by Dr. Ricardo Frazer

cs cs cs

REFERENCES

Achterberg, J. (1988). The wounded healer transformational journeys in modern medicine. In G. Doore, (Ed.), *Shaman's path: Healing, personal growth and empowerment* (pp.115-125). Boston: Shambhala.

Adams, T.B., Bezner, J.R., Drabbs, M.E., Zambarano, R.J., & Steinhardt M.A. (2000). Conceptualization and measurement of the spiritual and psychological dimensions of wellness in a college population. *Journal of American College Health, 48*, 165-173.

Adler, A. (1929). *The practice and theory of individual psychology* (P. Radin. Trans.). New York: Harcourt, Brace, and Company.

Ardell, D.B. (1977). High level wellness strategies. *Health Education, 8*, 2-4.

Bailey, C.W. (2000). *God, Dr. Buzzard, and the Bolito man: A saltwater Geechee talks about life on Sapelo Island, Georgia.* New York: Anchor Books.

Bandura, A. (1977). Self-efficacy: Toward a unifying theory of behavioral change *Psychological Review, 84* (2), 191-215.

Bernard, C.P. (1994). Resiliency: A shift in our perception? *American Journal of Family Therapy, 22* (2), 135-144.

Bucke, R.M. (2009). *Cosmic consciousness.* New York: Dover Publications.

Chopra, D. (1994). *The seven spiritual laws of success: A practical guide to the fulfillment of your dreams.* California: Aber-Allen Publishing.

Cross, W.E. (1971). The Negro-to-Black conversion experience: Towards a psychology of black liberation. *Black World, 20*, 13-27.

Csikszentmihalyi, M. (1990). *Flow: The psychology of optimal experience.* New York: Harper Perennial Modern Classics.

Dunn, H.L. (1977). *High-level wellness.* Thorofare: NJ: Charles B. Slack.

Egbert, E. (1980). Concept of wellness. *Journal of Psychiatric Nursing and Mental Health Services*, 9-13.

Eliade, M. (1964). Shamanism: Archaic techniques of ecstasy. London: Arkana Penguin Books.

Erikson, E. (1950). *Childhood and society.* New York: W.W. Norton and Company.

Erikson, E.H., Paul, I.H., Heider, F., & Garder, R.W. (1959). *Psychological issues* (Vol.1). New York: International Universities Press.

Frazer, R.A. (2011). *Psychological wellness and holistic health care: The Karmu System.* Indiana: Xlibris.

Giler, J.Z. (1981). Karmu as wounded healer. *Unpublished Master's Thesis:* California State University.

Giler, J.Z. (2012). *Karmu Urban Shaman.* CES Amazon. Ebook.

Greenberg, J.S. (1985). Health and wellness: A conceptual differentiation. *Journal of School Health, 55*, 403-406.

Gropp, L. (2006). *An exploratory factor analysis on the measurements of psychological wellness.* Pretoria: Unisa.

Gropp, L., Geldenhuys, D., & Visser, D. (2007). Psychological wellness construct: Relationships and group differences. *South African Journal of Industrial Psychology, 33* (3), 24-34.

Hanley, M.S. & Noblit, G.W. (2009). Cultural responsiveness, racial identity, and academic success: A review of literature. *The Heinz Endowments:* Pennsylvania.

Henderson, N. (1997). Resiliency in schools: Making it happen. *Principal, 77* (2), 10-17.

Hettler, B. (1980). Wellness promotion on a university campus: Family and community health. *Journal of Health Promotion and Maintenance, 3*, 77-95.

Hill, N.R. (2004). The challenges experienced by pre-tenured faculty members in counseling education: A wellness perspective. *Counselor Education and Supervision, 44*, 135-146.

Jung, C. (1968). *Analytical psychology: Its theory and practice.* New York: Vintage Books.

Kloss, J. (1939). *Back to Eden: A human interest story of health and restoration to be found in herb, root, and bark.* WI: Lotus Press.

Maslow, A.H. (1964). *Religions, values, and peak experiences.* London: Penguin Books Limited.

Maslow, A.H. (1968). *Toward a psychology of being* (2nd ed.). New York: Van Nostrand.

Maslow, A.H. (1971). *The farther reaches of human nature.* New York: Viking.

Myers, L. (1988). *An Afrocentric worldview: Introduction to an optimal psychology.* Dubuque, IA: Kendall-Hunt.

Nicolaus, G. (2011). *C.G. Jung and Nikolai Berdyaev: Individuation and the person, a critical comparison.* New York; Routledge.

Rogers, C. (1961). *On becoming a person: A therapist's view of psychotherapy.* Boston: Houghton Mifflin Company.

Roscoe, L. (2009). Wellness: A review of theory and measurement for counselors. *Journal of Counseling & Development, 87,* 216-226.

Schwarzer, R. (2008). Modeling health behavior change: How to predict and modify the adoption and maintenance of health behaviors. *Applied Psychology: An International Review, 57* (1), 1–29.

Seligman, M., & Csikszentmihalyi, M. (2000). Positive psychology: An introduction. *American Psychologist, 55,* 5-14.

Sellers, R. & Shelton, J. (2003). The role of racial identity in perceived racial discrimination. *Journal of Personality and Social Psychology, 88* (5), 1079-1092.

Snook, J. & Oliver, M. (2015). Perceptions of wellness from adults with mobility impairments. *Journal of Counseling & Development, 93,* 289-298.

Sulliman, J.R. (1973). The development of a scale for the measurement of social interest. *Dissertation Abstracts International, 34*/06, B2914.

Stevens J. (1987). *Storming heaven: LSD and the American dream.* New

York: Grove Press.

Thompson, S., & Chambers, J. (2000). African self-consciousness and health-promoting behaviors among African American college students. *Journal of Black Psychology, 26* (3), 330-345.

Van Eeden, C. (1996). *Psigologiese welstand en koherensin.* Ongepubliseerd Ph.D. Tesis, Potchefstroom: PU vir CHO.

Wallis, S.E. (2010). Towards a science of metatheory. *Integral Review, 6*(3), 73-120.

Walsh, R., & Shapiro, D. H. (1983). *Beyond health and normality: Explorations of exceptional psychological well-being.* New York; Van Notstrand Reinhold.

Warner, E. (1977). *Karmu is a Healer: A book to serve as a companion in time of sickness and health.* Cambridge: A Church of Karmu Publication.

 Cʒ Cʒ Cʒ